TOYING WITH

Love

With Love Series: BookOne

Caron Prins & Tish Ings

Copyright © 2018 Caron Prins & Tish Ings

All rights reserved.

ISBN-13: 978-1-988700-64-9

DEDICATION
AND
ACKNOWLEDGMENTS

From *Caron Prins*

To my Achacha sister. Thank you for saying yes. From the bottom of my heart, only you will know how much. With Love.

From *Tish Ings*

Anything for you, sissy. I'll always say yes when you ask, no matter what. I love you!

CHAPTER ONE

"This is for *him*, ladies."

Pam, the petite brunette *Desire By Design* saleslady whipped out a fully erect, six-inch silicone dildo and slammed the suction cup attached to the display table already covered in her merchandise. The bright pink offering vibrated from the impact, settling into a swaying wave at the women in the crowd.

I gaped, mouth open, snapping it shut when the visual of my parted lips and that particular item made a mental connection that brought a deep blush to my cheeks. "It's *what*?" I think that was what I said. Since I struggled to connect my logical brain to my tongue in that moment, I could have merely gurgled something incoherent.

Not that anyone noticed. Gasps and shocked faces followed my lead, women all over the room erupting into giggles after the initial shock of such blatant exposure. Except, of course, my bestie and the reason I was here in the first place. All teeth, boobs and eyes, Jones laughed, doubling over in an attack of epic hilarity at my reaction, no doubt. I turned on her and her clearly delighted reaction to my prudish response to find her slapping her leg.

"Did she just say...?" For *him*? Was she serious? I couldn't even imagine it for me, let alone any guy I might date. Thinking about my ex-husband, Richard, even considering including such a toy in the bedroom made me want to laugh as loudly as Jones, but not for the same reason. More with a longing-filled kind of "I wish" than any actual humor.

Yes, I was still pining for him and a big enough girl to admit it.

Pam smiled sweetly, perfect lips slick with pink gloss, with a level of innocence indicative of someone looking to make a statement, used to dealing with aghast and yet titillated women who had previously only dreamed of holding a plastic dick in their hands.

"Oh, ladies, no. My apologies. This isn't for him after all. No, this is for *you*." As she spoke, she casually opened a tall, plastic box, the top popping with a jaunty joy that definitely lured my mind deeper into the show. Or was it just the proximity to a fake penis, vibrators and other sexual paraphernalia that made everything she said, did and held seem like the biggest innuendo in the world?

Within a moment of her twisting the top off the bottle she freed from the box, the scent of pomegranate hit my nose. While my inner innocent shivered in shame, warring with the tingling excitement of even considering repeating her actions, she poured a large dollop of what had to be lubricant onto the palm of her hand.

No one said a word, every one of us locked into staring as she then slowly and deliberately, a tiny, wicked smile on her lips, rubbed her palms together, long, fake nails shining as they encountered the gel. Her action helped the aroma disperse further into the room and, oddly, triggered hunger.

She must have known she had us, because she made no attempt to hurry, her actions confident but rather languid, as if she enjoyed every moment she spent luring us into her show. I tore my gaze from what she was doing long enough to note that, yes, aside from Jones who still chuckled to herself, not a single woman in the room seemed able to focus anywhere but the saleswoman and her proudly erect pink friend.

I caught the lady next to me sliding closer to the front of her seat and resisted the urge to do the same, forcing my clenched hands to release my death grip on my wine glass. With a deep breath, I sternly reminded myself I was a grown woman. It wasn't like I was some virginal teenager who'd never seen a penis before. All fine and good, except, of course, as the rep reached with her slicked hands for the waving dildo I actually caught the hysterical giggle threatening at the back of my throat before it could emerge and embarrass me.

My only consolation was knowing I was hardly alone in feeling so captivated.

Without warning, Pam grabbed her partner in crime and started to work her hands up and down, so effortlessly, talking while she massaged the dildo like it was a real man. "You can take him anywhere, really ladies. In your car, in the shower, even take him to work." That last suggestion she made with a huge grin and a wink that triggered a group laugh, nervous and yet excited at the same time. Even I found myself snorting, blushing all over again at the thought of hiding such a prize in my purse and finding time to take advantage of it at my desk.

Was it embarrassing or interesting I realized her technique was actually intriguing? Richard's preferences always leaned toward him on top and not a lot of nonsense—his

4

favorite term for foreplay. Something I'd gotten used to over the years we'd spent together. But she made it seem like taking her time to actually handle the dildo might actually be fun.

Yes, I knew what porn was. No, I wasn't a fan. Everyone knew it was fake. So all of the so-called sex moves I'd ever considered felt about as real as the garbage I'd encountered over the years. I couldn't help but wonder, though, what it might actually feel like.

Pam rotated the penis expertly, switching from hand to hand. At the top she twisted her wrist, completing a 360 on the head before sliding out of the way for the other hand to take over.

"Ask her if you can try." Jones hadn't lost her sense of humor, pale blue eyes twinkling. I smacked her knee with one hand, knowing I was blushing all over again, while Pam wrapped up her demo, wiping her hands on a small towel before winking at me.

Please, don't address me directly. I would have sunk through the floor, I was sure of it. Thankfully, instead, she reached into the large, black bag at her side and retrieved yet another box. "No, ladies, *this* is for him." Out popped a light pink silicone tube, about the size of my fist, maybe five inches in length. I could almost feel the women around me twitch to pay closer attention.

"What is that?" Someone murmured it, but I knew we were all wondering, like the sexual tension in the room created some sort of collective consciousness. Pam upended the delicious smelling gel and poured a generous dollop into the pink cylinder. "What's the worst thing about blowjobs?" She asked so innocently, without a hint of self-consciousness and I found my own dissipating because of her confidence.

Not so everyone, though. The women around me seemed more nervous, not less, giggling like teenagers. Until someone from the back piped up with her words slurring slightly from the abundant flow of wine we'd all been offered to soften us up.

"Hairy balls?"

That, of course, set the whole flock of women into laughter, me included, Jones the loudest, her jet black hair falling over one shoulder as she crumpled forward over her knees.

Laughing herself, Pam answered her own question. "Gagging, am I right?" She really went there? I flinched, sitting back, remembering the few times I'd tried to give Richard what he wanted. I couldn't take the pressure against the back of my throat, almost throwing up. That had put an end to me trying so he finally quit asking. Pam went on while shame lit my cheeks all over again. Maybe this was a terrible idea after all. I didn't need to be reminded about how disappointed he'd been. I was already divorced, thanks. "And yes, hairy balls."

More laughter, but this time as I pulled myself out of memory, I could see the others were more on high alert. As if their comfort level increased this time while mine seemed on a rapid retreat.

"Meet Madame Kitty." Pam's hands grasped the pink toy firmly. "This little gem will be your new best friend the next time your man asks you to go down on him." She pulled slowly, stretching the silicone until it paled in color. "You can use it to simulate a hand job." She lowered one end over the dildo on the table, sliding the lubricated sleeve over top of the head and devoured the whole penis in a split second. As she continued to explain, her hands never stopped moving, working the soft sleeve up and down. "Or, you can pleasure him orally, but now, thanks to Madame Kitty, all you have to work on is this." She pushed the toy down to the bottom of the shaft, revealing only a couple of inches of hard flesh exposed with the tip standing at attention. "No more gagging."

Maybe I was being indoctrinated by her casual approach, but that was kind of awesome. From the murmurs of appreciation and eager expressions, I wasn't the only one who thought so. Pam was going to sell quite of few Madame Kitty's tonight. Too bad I didn't have anyone to share it with.

And there was the self-pity again, the very same pity Jones was so sick of she dragged me here tonight, to this crazy party. Feeling sorry for myself firmly in check, I listened as Pam went on.

"And," she said, retrieving the toy from the dildo, "if he's being an ass," she bounced the tube of silicone in her hand before pretending to chuck it across the room, she said, "you can throw it at him and tell him to take care of himself."

A roar of laughter and applause rewarded her suggestion. Pam, once more wiping her hands on a fresh towel, allowed the chatter to die down, all smiles as she waited us out. The nervous giggling finally subsided, enough Pam had our full attention again. She gave a little bow in her seat before meeting each of our eyes while she wrapped up her demonstration. "Now, I'll be in the other room where I'm set up for any questions and purchases." Gazes flickered to the closed bedroom door on the other side of the living room. I'd never been to this apartment before, the hostess a friend of Jones's, but I'd drifted past before Pam started her presentation, telling myself there was no way I'd be going in there to buy anything, that this was Jones's idea of a joke. Only now? I was actually considering at least talking to Pam.

Wouldn't hurt, right? Besides, this was research, in a way. For my book. Writing a hot romance would be a lot more fun if I had some props to inspire me, wouldn't it?

Pam wasn't done. She must have known some of us would be reticent because her expression softened from wicked teasing to utter professionalism. "Let me assure you, every purchase is done in private, and with the utmost discretion. If you don't want to show off your new toys, you don't have to. Everything about tonight from this moment on is about you, for you, and totally up to you. Any interaction with me is completely confidential."

I sat back, staring into my almost empty glass of Merlot, holding still while Pam rose and exited the living room, murmuring something to the hostess before disappearing behind the bedroom door.

CHAPTER TWO

An elbow landed in my ribs, making me jump. I turned to Jones before she could make a wisecrack, her favorite, and grasped her hand.

"Thank you for bringing me here tonight." Did I mean it? I actually did. "I really needed this." I actually felt good about the whole thing. I'd made it through a sex toy party and the world hadn't imploded. I was even on my way to a bit more open to the whole idea. Who would have thought?

Jones wasn't going to let me off easy, though. "You mean thank you for dragging you here kicking and screaming?"

I would have protested except, of course,

she was right. She literally walked into my apartment with the spare key I gave her and bullied me into getting changed from my sweats into a dress while drinking half of the Riesling I had in the fridge. It was probably best she hadn't told me where we were going.

"I'm glad you came." She poked me again, finishing off her own glass of wine with a deep sigh, free hand tugging the silky length of her straight, dark hair out of her way. I always wished I had the courage to wear tight t-shirts like she did, usually white with bright pink or blue or some other wild color lace bra showing clearly through, too much cleavage for polite company a trademark as much as her full but slender build. "You need to be reminded that the world doesn't begin and end with The Dick."

Richard had hated it when Jones called him that. With good reason. I'd taken to using it in my own head, though, I had to admit, when I was angry with him. Not that I'd ever call him that to his face, or anything. But the times I still floundered around his infidelity with the stereotypical younger woman.

Could I even be more of a cliché?

I swallowed a mouthful of wine so I didn't have to speak right away, the familiar tightening in the back of my throat warning of tears. I'd found out he was cheating over six months ago. I really needed to get over it, already. But I guess I wasn't the getting over fast type or something, nor really in the party girl mood.

When I met Jones's eyes, she winked. And I caught myself smiling back, a real smile for once, not a forced one I used to try to fool her and myself into thinking I was okay. I really was grateful. Where would I have been without Jones? Still at home, in my sweats, crying over a pint of ice cream and a bottle of wine. Instead, in walked my BFF demanding I come back to the world. And her.

Enough was enough. "Okay, Jones," I said, setting aside my glass, stomach tight with anxiety but decision made. "You're right. Time to put my big girl pants back on and move on."

Instead of saying I told you so, Jones just grinned, nodded, accepted and trusted me. Could I have loved her more in that moment? I doubted it. Without her tough, don't fuck with me strength, paired with her huge heart, would take all your pain from you if she could, Jones's simple smile was the epitome of everything that made her awesome.

She was everything I wished I could be. I loved her for it but also had the courage to admit I envied her, big time.

"I've got a great idea." Jones was on fire, I could see it in her eyes. "Let's get the most ridiculous gaudy toys we can find and take them to *Sparkle*." I wasn't sure I wanted to know what her plan was, or how it involved her usual night club, though my imagination stirred more nervous laughter. "We carry them around, bold as you please, dance with them, drink with them." I almost choked on the image. "And when anyone says anything? We tell them they are our new boyfriends, the best we have ever had." Jones belly laughed, drawing attention from the other, now quieter ladies who waited their turn to visit Pam in the bedroom. I shushed her, but she ignored me. Because, of course, she was Jones, and such a suggestion was utterly acceptable.

She had to have known she'd get pushback from me. Honestly, she couldn't even convince me to wear the dress she'd forced me to buy, the red one the handsome and very gay salesman told me screamed, "Just take me, already." Even the thought of showing off high thigh made me queasy. But Jones wasn't about to quit now while she was on a roll. She grabbed me and hauled me to my feet, dragging me toward the open bar set up near the kitchen. "First, we have a bottle of someone else's wine each. Then we dance the night away. You in, sista?"

My hesitation wasn't doing it for her, nor my not-so-subtle tugging against the firm grasp she had on my wrist. "Mick." At least she didn't call me Michaela. She only did that when she was ready to chew me out. Mick meant she was still in a good mood. "What is it now? You know you always have fun after the pain of me forcing you to have some." She was right, though more often than not I ended up leaving early or embarrassed and hiding behind her when she flirted with two men at a time in an effort to get one of them interested in me. "So, what the fuck?"

Normally, I would have made an excuse and begged off. Being here tonight, in the company of other women far more like me than like her, gave me a bit more courage to speak up. "I'm not like that, Jones. I'm not like you."

She tossed her hands, frustration clear on her gorgeous face, tightening her big, pale eyes, sending dots of bright pink to the heights of her arching cheekbones. Compared to me with my red hair and freckles, Jones was an exotic goddess. No wonder she found this easy. I was just me. "Mickey, woman, for once can you stop thinking for a change and go with the flow?" Did she have any idea how crazy that sounded? "You won't end up in jail or anything." She snorted. "At least, not alone." Great, thanks for that. "And you won't die. Just lighten up, damn it." Jones looked down at the wine bottles, hesitated and then looked up at last, her own eyes rimmed with moisture. "I miss you."

I hated hurting her. She was the only

person in my life who didn't judge me, who tried to encourage me. I was right on the edge of losing it in that stranger's living room, clutching at my empty glass of wine while my best friend fought tears for me, for us.

I knew she was right, that was the worst part. It was impossible not to hate myself for dragging her along on my pity party. Though, a little part of me rebelled, still feeding off the fact I wasn't the minority, that she was the rarity here in this room.

"Just back off, please." I couldn't believe I actually said that to her, saw her flinch, fall uncomfortably still. I should have stopped, maybe, but I couldn't, the words gushing out, low enough at least it was just the two of us but made worse, maybe, from the intimacy of our connection. "You know better than anyone what I've just gone through. And that I'm trying. But I need time."

Jones didn't say anything for a moment. When she did, her tone had changed from jovial good humor to flat frustration. "Mick, girlfriend, you need to take your power back." Okay, now I wasn't listening because she hadn't heard a word I said. But Jones wasn't done, doing her best to boss me around now, instead of being a friend. "This keeping in touch bullshit and being Richard's errand girl isn't helping you get on with your life."

I looked away, hurt running deep. Yes,

okay, so I did my best to stay friends with Richard, for both our sakes. We'd spent a lot of years together, had a relationship. I wasn't willing to just throw that away, despite his cheating. Other women grew bitter and badmouthed their exes. I wasn't going to be that woman. The opposite, in fact. I was his friend and if I helped him out with things he needed from time to time, well that made me a good person. Better than most of the divorced women I knew.

Jones's expression softened but that didn't help my mood. If anything, her attitude made things worse. Because that pity she now shared, held deep in her eyes? That told me she judged me for the choices I'd made. And she didn't get to judge, not with the lifestyle she lived.

I took a deep breath, smothered my resentment, the surge of anger toward her. I would not be the one to end our friendship, not when I loved her as much as I did. Jones was trying to help. She just didn't understand that Richard still needed me sometimes and that part of my closure was being a good person. Maybe if he saw how I treated him he'd learn to be a better man, too.

Jones helped herself to a swig of wine right from a bottle, swinging it in my direction a moment later. "You're too good for him," she said. "He didn't even wait a month before he was engaged to that piece of trash he cheated with. And their sham of a wedding six weeks later? Come on, Mick. Wake the hell up."

He told me it had been her idea, his new wife, that she gave him no choice. And I believed him. It was all her, anyway. She'd seduced him. My fault, too, for not giving him what he wanted. I was going to be the good person here, even if it killed me.

Jones wasn't done. "You're beautiful, smart, and funny, usually, and your ass is perfect. You have gone so far up Richard's anus into all his shit you don't see your worth anymore." Wow, that was blunt, and I was used to Jones. "You literally accept shit because you are covered in it."

I spluttered. I don't think I've ever actually spluttered before, but I did as my mind fired off in anger. Instead of reacting with her own fury, though, satisfaction woke on Jones's face. She set down the bottle in her hand, gaze flickering over my shoulder, as she grasped my upper arms and spun me forcefully around. I found myself propelled toward the now open bedroom door, a few women lingering close but not entering, Jones hot on my heels.

"Take that pent up fire and get your hot tush in there, missy, and don't you dare leave the room without something fun and all for you." She slapped my ass as I moved to do what she said, still struggling to argue with her while crossing the threshold.

I turned around with surprise and a little start, cheek stinging from the strike of her hand through my jeans. That felt better than it was supposed to, though there was no way I would ever tell her that. The thought that maybe I did need something to keep me company at night loomed in the back of my mind while the bedroom door slammed in my face.

CHAPTER THREE

The sales rep waited for me, perched on the edge of the bed, her long, tanned legs crossed, designer heel bobbing on the end of one narrow foot. Her smile seemed welcoming enough, though I wondered in the back of my mind if she ever poked internal fun at the endless line of women who came to her makeshift store of goodies laid out in precise rows on the carefully made bed.

Honestly, it was about as brilliant as it was fitting, this display of sexual wares on a queen sized mattress. Did she know or was the choice hers? She had to know, didn't she?

As my mind struggled with the winding thoughts that carried me as far from what I was about to do as possible, drawing out enough logic I was able to inhale and then exhale without passing out from the embarrassment of knowing the rest of the women waiting for their turn were well aware what I was up to right now, at this moment. What were they thinking I was doing in here? Testing the merch for quality? Yikes. More likely speculating what I was going to buy. Guessing that I was all kinds of dirty.

Let them. It would be, after all, their go shortly.

"Great presentation." I attempted a smile, trying for light and inconspicuous and likely coming across as awkwardly pathetic. Didn't help that my judgments and thoughts almost made me run, hightail it for the door and my ordinary, boring, sexless life. That train to nowhere was enough to stop me from beating a retreat. At least long enough for Pam to speak up.

"Please come in." As if I wasn't already standing there, trapped between the lineup of dildos and toys and the door. Maybe if she wasn't so sweet and ever so professional I might have actually bolted. Instead, feeling my heartrate settle into something that wasn't going to lead to pending failure in 3-2-1, I eased my way forward, realizing only then I had my back pressed to the door.

"First time?" She gestured at her wares,

turning up the wattage on her smile. "There's nothing to be nervous about, I promise. Everything we discuss is private and discreet. I'm here to make sure you're satisfied with your sexuality."

Wow, she had no idea how big a job she had ahead of her.

I looked down at the bed, a mistake for my already spinning brain. Overwhelm struck me right away, triggering my favorite response, verbal diarrhea. "I don't know what I want, I mean I've never used anything other than natural and that's not that great, but now I'm divorced and I haven't really had an orgasm before and I wouldn't even know where to start, I mean I know where to start.... I think I do, but do they all have batteries?"

Pam's smile didn't falter, even when I ground to an embarrassing and stuttering halt, feeling my cheeks heat, my whole body waver while I vaguely considered throwing up. Why was I so nervous? I had to keep reminding myself I was a grown woman as Pam stood up and approached me, offering one hand. I took it on autopilot and squeezed instantly back when she gently pressed her fingers against mine before letting me go.

"Why don't we start with what you like when it comes to pleasure and I'll make suggestions to get you started?"

I was expecting teasing, even a bit of sass.

Not kindness, the sort of compassion that utterly shook me and yet drew me out at the same time. "I have no idea where to start."

She nodded, smiled again and, in that moment, I learned to trust her. Funny how you can endear yourself to someone just by paying attention. I had no idea I was so starving to be heard. Quite the realization at a time like that in a situation like this and over a collection of sex toys that had nothing to do with the depth of thought and emotion passing through me.

Or did they?

Pam's demeanor stayed steady, kindly, her professionalism kicking in again. "I have certain recommendations for first toys, but do you know what experience you would like to have?" I didn't answer, trying to remember what it was like with Richard. And snorted that away. Memories of his weight on me, of the discomfort of him inside me, over before I could find any real satisfaction while he rolled off and fell asleep, just made me sad. It wasn't like I didn't know better, right? The one time I'd decided to see if the erotica I'd read was right and did a bit of experimentation in the tub, touching certain sensitive parts, ended in panting and more frustration when the expected rush of whatever it was "they" said I was supposed to experience didn't happen.

Maybe I was just incapable. That meant this was a waste of time.

Pam's voice broke through my spiral into despair I was somehow broken. "Soft, medium or hard?"

Before I could comprehend what that even meant, she leaned down to the bed and lifted a short, pink dildo, the shape a perfect penis as if some man had his private parts cast into a mold as the model. For all I knew, one had. She placed it carefully in my open palm and closed my fingers around it. At once fascinated and slightly aroused—it was just silicone, sheesh, what was wrong with my body all of a sudden?—I let myself feel the weight and the flexible silk of it against my skin.

"This is soft," she said. "Firm enough for insertion, but smaller and without complete rigidity. Excellent to start with, though I recommend lube, as with all my toys."

As she spoke I stared down at the fake dick in my hands and almost choked on a laugh. Even as my brain clicked and I realized I wasn't going to die of embarrassment after all and yes, I could do this.

"I think soft would be best." I met her eyes, noting I loved her makeup application as I scrambled for a distraction, wishing I had the steady hand to make those perfect cat eyes with a liquid liner and that she somehow managed to apply mascara without clumps. Surely a woman worthy of my trust.

Pam's nose scrunched, adorable. "Well, let's

look at this dolphin." The penis disappeared and she set another in my hand, this one blue with a tiny, I kid you not, dolphin shape rising out of the tinted silicone, arching upward as if it were leaping from a wave. "It's the perfect first timer toy." She flipped the switch on the bottom as she set it in my hand, the vibration making my skin shiver. "This will stimulate your clitoris and help you achieve a wonderful orgasm." She said the "O" word with such ease I didn't even flinch, fingers tingling from the change in vibration as she adjusted the speed with a small remote control. "It's super easy to use. And he's waterproof, so bath time can be even more relaxing." The reminder of my failed attempt almost did me in, but Pam wasn't done talking. "Just think of it as a massager for your clitoris. You get body massages don't you?"

"Yes," I said. This was no different. Keep telling yourself that, Mickey.

"So why not invest in a massager for pleasure?" Pam switched it off but didn't take it from me, letting me hold the blue penis with the dolphin rising from the wave.

You know what? She was so right. I clung to the tiny toy like it was breath while my body made up my mind for me.

"I'll take it. Thank you."

Just like that she had my credit card, swiping it through the reader attached to her smartphone, and I was the proud owner of a blue dolphin dildo vibrator complete with remote control and a free pack of batteries to get me started.

Standing there, staring at the little slip of paper proving I now owned my very first vibrator, buyer's remorse jabbed me with instant regret. What was I thinking? This was going to show up on my credit card statement. What would the bank think? And Richard would see it. Wait, no he wouldn't. We weren't married anymore. We had our own accounts, our own cards now. He had no say in what I did.

Pam guided me toward the door, while I gaped at her with the obvious question as I headed for the exit empty handed. "Your purchase will arrive at your door by special delivery in the next day or so. Don't worry, the company is completely discreet and uses only plain cardboard packaging. You don't have to do a thing, but please let me know if you have any questions or problems with your products." Her card settled in my hand before she opened the door. "Thank you, and enjoy the rest of your evening." Only then did she let me leave, smiling and gesturing for the next customer in line. The older woman with the heavy makeup and nails shaped like talons laughed out loud before hurrying to take my place, the door thudding shut behind her.

CHAPTER FOUR

I spotted Jones right away as I exited the sales room, talking to someone I didn't recognize. I really didn't care to meet anyone new at that moment anyway and had a sneaking suspicion the collection of women whose party we'd joined weren't exactly friends of hers. It would be just like Jones to drop us uninvited into someone else's gathering on a whim and a whisper of fun. I was used to it enough I knew to hide behind her charm and charisma and just let her do her thing so we didn't get kicked out.

Right now, though, I just wanted out, fresh air, a chance to breathe after the intensity of oh my god, what did I just do? I dodged her and ducked toward the front door of the condo where the hostess was saying goodbye to others. I took my place in that queue and followed like I was a part of their pack. I couldn't even remember her name, though I quickly kissed her cheek and forced a thank you before dodging around the others who had stopped to yammer words I couldn't even comprehend just then.

By the time I reached the corridor on my way outside I couldn't seem to get enough oxygen in my lungs, darkness closing in around the edges, hyperventilation threatening to do the unspeakable and drive me into a honest-to-goodness fainting spell. It wasn't until I made it into the street, the heavy, hydrocarbon and faintly garbage-tinged atmosphere that permeated the city that I was able to actually catch myself and retreat from the impending need to pass out.

Thank goodness for pollution and the jarring honk of passing cars. I always felt like the city blanketed me, protecting me with in a wash of anonymity. Passing pedestrians, their faces down over the screens of their phones or their lips locked on a coffee cup even this late at night, tiny dogs on leashes trailing them over the rattling metal covers to the under street storage while the subway hummed past through the grates in the pavement all tied together with the rush of noisy traffic to settle me back into the reality of one girl, one soul, giant city.

Just a ten minute subway ride and I could forget all about tonight. I hit the sidewalk with knees just getting their strength back, firming up further when I descended the stairs into the subway tunnel and moved through the carousel on my way to the platform, a few passengers joining me while the rush of air and the rumble of the exiting train told me I was just in time to catch my ride. Luck on my side, I slipped on board, sliding in the first seat closest to the door as the few other travelers took their own places to the whoosh of the doors closing.

I kept my head down, eyes locked on the compressed floor of the car, hands folded in my lap, not wanting to draw attention to myself, though the train was nearly empty. Just how I liked it. The next stop filled the car further, shuffling feet passing my sight line. The final passenger staggered, sank into the seat next to me while I cringed and slid sideways wishing he'd chosen someone else to torture with his manspreading. I did my best not to react while his wide-open knees pushed against my thigh and the scent of alcohol on his breath made me gag.

"Hey, beautiful lady." Great, one of those. I didn't respond, knew better than to say a word or to look up for any kind of help from other passengers. One of the trials of taking the subway, unfortunately. "What you doing on here all by yourself? You want company?"

I made the mistake of glancing sideways, but I couldn't help it. His hand was moving and the motion caught my attention. Horrified but unable to react, I was forced to watch him rub the front of his jeans. Okay, not forced, not really, but I couldn't help it. Talk about witnessing a train wreck and not being able to look away.

I heard him chuckle as I jerked my eyes back to the floor, face flaming. At least someone was enjoying himself, if the way he'd grown in his pants was any indication. I could report him to the transit cops. Even turn with my phone and snap his photo, maybe get him banned. I'd seen brave women do so, braver than me. Thing was, there were a million men like him, so what good would it do? Instead of drawing attention to myself further, I kept my head down. If I didn't react, he'd get tired of his game and leave.

Except he didn't seem like he was ready to go just yet. The instant the train pulled into the next stop I was up and off, exhaling into the stale, stinking air of the underground while new passengers pushed past me on their way to board, hoping he didn't follow. I glanced behind me while I hurried to the steps and exhaled in relief when there was no sign of him. I paused at the sight of a pair of transit police in their dark blue uniforms, considered reporting the creep, then sagged and sighed and left.

As I emerged into the open air, the sounds of the city engulfing me again, I felt a tingle of anger at myself, frustration rising all over again. I'd been forced off the train two stops early, but there was no way I was going back on board tonight. Instead, I decided to walk, taking the sidewalk by storm. Well, in all honesty, keeping to myself, hands in my pockets, head down, turning sideways to avoid running into more aggressive pedestrians while my mind complained at me.

It was hard not to devolve into thinking about the last fifteen years and where my life was now. Almost impossible not to think of Richard. Yes, he cheated, Jones was right. But I had to take some kind of responsibility for the end of my marriage, in the fact Richard felt his only recourse was to find someone else. Maybe I pushed him away. I really wanted children and he was adamant he wasn't having any. I spent years thinking he would change his mind when we got married. But, no. Had I forced him away because of my selfishness?

The realization of my life of cliché, now thirty-seven and too old to have kids, that I'd wasted my best years on a man who didn't want me or what I wanted, was about as unexpected as this whole night's revelations and actually stopped me in my tracks.

My life sucked. I hated him with a surge of rage and vitriol, hated he'd ruined my life. What was I going to do now?

As fast as that hate woke, it died. My fault, as much as his. All I could do now was make the best of it.

I arrived at my building in a fog. A brief moment of interest woke as I spotted two uniformed police officers talking to my downstairs neighbor, the sight of her ransacked apartment on the other side of her open door and her tear-stained face telling me she'd been unlucky tonight. There had been a rash of break ins in our neighborhood, but since I didn't have anything to take, really, I tried not to worry. Besides, I told myself as I took the endless flights to my apartment slower than usual when the closed for repairs sign on the elevator made me pant my way home, what self-respecting thief would rob a place six floors up?

I hit the landing with a heavy sigh and shoulders bearing the weight of the world, eyes locked on the carpet, feet carrying me to my green painted door with the brass 614. My key slipped in the lock, mind on autopilot, the light switch beside the entry responding as usual with the familiar flare of light overhead. The ceramic bowl I'd haphazardly made in a short class last year rattled with the drop of my keyring, wobbling on its uneven bottom.

At least someone was there to greet me. Zeus waited on the counter in the kitchen, little thick arms jaunty, pinpoints of spines dark against his small, green cactusness. I paused and tried a smile at the little plant Jones gave me as a freedom housewarming. The Little Prick, she called him with a laugh. I took one look at his dry soil and sighed. How could I possibly have thought I could raise kids when I couldn't even keep a damn plant alive?

Dragging my sorry ass off to bed, not even washing my face, I crawled under the covers and laid back. I had so many conversations going on in my head, how was it I felt so alone? Sleep finally took me after the latest heroine fight/plea succeeded and I finally convinced Richard that we were meant to be together and no one could separate us ever again.

Before I opened my eyes in the early morning light, before I could collect my thoughts or protect myself against her, I heard Jones's voice in my head.

You got this, kid. Pull up your big girlies and seize the day.

I wanted to argue, but even without her

actually here to say it out loud, her words had weight. Yes, you pushy, bossy brat of a friend. She was right, though mental Jones sounded a lot like the self-help guru whose hypnosis program hadn't done much except take money from my bank account. Still, I had a choice, right? Today was a new day. I would be the best me I could be today. And no one going to stop me.

I swung out of bed, optimism firmly in place, just as my phone chimed a text and the inevitability of my existence reminded me optimism wasn't on the menu.

Richard needed me. Of course.

CHAPTER FIVE

My heart clenched from emotional body memory, tensing for a blow that never actually landed. I never received texts this early unless it was Richard and he needed something. And he did this morning, though as I found myself walking through the glass door into Mike's Drycleaners, I had to admit it felt almost surreal, as if someone else had read the panicked text about his need for his power shirt for the "Big Day" court case he was involved in, had leaped at the chance to do him this one teensy favor, like the woman who still needed him to validate her wasn't living in my head.

For the first time since our divorce, since I softened about his cheating, since I started to explain his behavior in terms of what I did wrong instead of the other way around, I asked myself the kind of question that stopped me in my tracks in the doorway, that made my heart pound a painful beat of awareness. Why was I the one my ex called when he needed something?

And, more importantly, why did I care again?

The young lady at the counter worked here for as long as I remembered, recognized me as I stumbled to the worn vinyl she leaned on, nodded to me with her usual perkiness. I'd always found Kim bubbly and kind and today was no exception.

"Here for the mister?" Had I told her we'd divorced? That thought never occurred to me and I found myself blushing as she spun and went for the turning rack, not even asking for my ticket. Good thing. Richard only gave me the number. She must have known exactly which one was his, though, because she returned an instant later, proffering the slippery bag with not one but three freshly cleaned shirts inside. "He called ahead," she rolled her eyes with a giggle, leaning over the counter far enough I had to avert my gaze or be privy to the color of her bra. Which always made me judge my own cleavage and found myself sadly lacking. I hated that my mind then spun toward wishing she'd just lean back again and show some propriety already.

Was I really that big of a prude? Or just jealous?

Kim grinned and winked, ringing in the order. I handed her my credit card, thinking with a start that the same card now carried the evidence of my clandestine purchase last night. I actually blushed again at the fact Richard's shirts and my vibrator shared digital space on my credit statement. I was so distracted by my private guilt I almost missed the fact she was rattling on like she always did, this time about school. But the word "journalism" caught and held my attention.

"I didn't know you were a writer." Yes, that was jealousy, fed by a kind of mad need to confess my own little secret. I'd always wanted to write, had been indulging that fantasy ever since I was a little girl. So I'd never actually done anything with the desire outside of talking about it with Jones, writing some fanfiction in a small group online to try to justify my Saturdays and Sundays spent at the keyboard while working on a book that never seemed to go anywhere. The fact this young woman with the bright eyes and impressive cleavage might actually be doing something I'd failed to do? As cringe worthy as it was enticing.

"I'm doing an online thing," she said, tossing that off as if being a writer wasn't an art, a calling. My first instinct was to dismiss her as one of *those*—someone who played at writing and didn't commit to it. Until I had to choke on my admission I was, too. Could today get any more depressing?

"So non-fiction?" Well, that was different. She wanted to blog or something. I had one of those already, even if it hadn't gone anywhere. Besides, I was a fiction author. Someone who didn't have to tell other people's real stories. I had the power to escape to any world I wanted. A great thing, especially for a lonely girl who was less important than what my parents were "discussing." Correction. It was usually my mom doing the discussing, my dad never raised his voice, was more of a lover than a fighter.

I snapped back, realizing I was drifting all over again, while Kim spoke. "It's super easy and wickedly fun." Her big, brown eyes blinked, heavy mascara making her lashes look bulky. "All I need to do is submit what I've observed in my every day. Kind of like being a fly on the wall. Keeping judgments out of it, you know? That's this week's assignment." It actually did sound fun, to be honest. "I just start writing and I hit a groove." She handed me back my credit card before tilting her head to one side, massive, dark curls bouncing over the shoulder of her tight, white t-shirt. "Do you write?"

Why was it so hard to respond? Instead of a casual, "yes," and leave it at that, Mickey, I instead stammered out, "I'm in the process of writing a novel. I like romance." More blushing. Great, now she'd think I was trashy or something. I'd heard talk about romance writers, left two critique groups because the other "serious" writers didn't take those kinds of books seriously. Like I cared. Except, apparently, I really did.

Instead of the reaction I was expecting, Kim beamed a smile at me. "That's awesome! I love romance, too." She sighed and tossed me a coy wink. "Must be easy to write, being married to Mr. O'Keefe and all." And that confirmed I'd never told her about the divorce. Though, a tiny part of my mind whispered Richard hadn't either, a little traitor of a spark that wondered why he'd stayed quiet. Kim giggled. "You're so lucky. He's super hot. I bet you've got some great scenes based on him, huh?"

My face felt robotic, tight, lips lifting into a smile I didn't ask for. No, I was too busy feeling like someone just drop kicked me. Instead of my typical stammer, though, I managed to shut up, wondering if Kim could see past the lie I wore all over my face.

I needed to correct her. To tell her Richard and I weren't together anymore, hadn't been for months. Instead, I turned and left with his shirts, my credit card in my hand instead of safely tucked in my wallet, disoriented and a bit numb. Was Jones right? Was I that pathetic I was still running around for Richard, not with him? In the hope there might be something, a spark, a possibility of our getting back together?

I refused to believe it, firmly controlling myself and my doubt as I stopped with purpose to put away my card, shuffling the shirts carefully so I didn't bunch them across my forearm and wrinkle them before I could make the delivery. Richard and I had a special relationship. We made sure of that. Sure, other ex-partners might not get along. But that didn't mean we couldn't, that friendship wasn't possible. I'd spent so many years with him, the thought of him leaving my life forever made my eyes burn, my throat tighten. Here I was, being the bigger person. By helping him out when he needed me, I was doing myself a service.

Because no way in hell was I bitter like my Mother and sister.

I flinched as I crossed the street. Why was I thinking about them? This had nothing to do with Mom or Tara, with my parent's failed marriage, with my sister's seemingly perfect union with her husband, her two perfect kids, her perfect life.

No, staying friends with Richard was about me, about making sure I remained a good person no matter what life threw at me. And in a way my continuing interactions were Mom's fault, right? Maybe if she stopped inviting him and his new wife over for dinner every Sunday. But no, it gave me a chance to prove to myself I could look beyond the past and let bygones be bygones. Made me strong, badass, right?

So why did I suddenly feel like I was on the verge of hyperventilating again? In less than twenty-four hours I'd felt deprived of oxygen to the point of passing out. I seriously needed to get a massive grip.

And besides, it was the price I paid to keep my family in my life and that was worth anything. My mother would be lost if I didn't come over for just the girl's dinner every Thursday, my one night of the week to spend time with her and my sister. I had to admit I was shocked and felt more than a little betrayed when Richard continued to come for family dinner. Mom insisted he would always remain part of the family and she was right. Besides, he was always so handsome and charming, one of the only people in her life that could make her laugh.

As I paused at the next light to wait for the walk sign, I wondered with a pinch of spite I quickly smothered with a sigh if Richard knew just what she was really like. My mother might have loved him to his face, but she could—and did—rip him to verbal shreds when he wasn't in the room. Impressive how that woman could do a one-eighty when he sweet talked her at the dinner table over stuffed chicken.

My feet thudded on the pavement as I crossed with the mass of people moving in the same direction, dodging and swearing softly under my breath when someone brushed against Richard's shirts. This was ridiculous, wasn't it? Every time I let myself think about the whole situation, I had to talk myself down from shaking anger that bubbled under my need to make everyone happy.

And, as I stopped again, the press of bodies close enough I could smell perfume, cologne, body odor while leaving me feeling completely and utterly alone in a mass of people who had no idea or care I was there, I made a decision. The kind of choice that crackled with giddy wonder and excitement, that triggered a nervous giggle and a shiver of rebellion.

It was time. This Sunday was my last. Now to find a way to tell my mother I was done having dinner with Richard and the woman he chose over me. Michaela Maria O'Keefe had enough.

CHAPTER SIX

Wow, where had this newfound sense of power come from? I slammed through the glass doors to my office building all pumped up and ready for anything, including a random sicko hitting on me, my mother's whining wrath or an alien invasion. The faster I walked, the closer to the elevator, the stronger the feeling grew. I caught myself smiling in the mirror between the silver doors, the sensation of a bubble around me, some kind of protective shield ready to guard me from any assault that might come my way so intense I actually smiled at the woman standing next to me. She smiled back, though she seemed nervous, so maybe I was riding too high.

No such thing. I march in throwing the shirt across the spare chair that's in my cubicle getting ready to tackle the day. A sharp smack on my ass turned me turn around to find my cubicle neighbor, Paul, grinning like the assault was funny. He'd shed his dark brown jacket and had rolled the sleeves of his beige shirt to his narrow elbows, the harsh light overhead shining on the thinned crown of his dark hair. I forced a smile back, knowing it was just his way of being friendly, but not in the mood at the moment.

"Hey," I said, wondering where my usual sense of affinity for him had gone. He was one of the only people in the office I could actually talk to.

"Looking some fine today, Michaela." Whether he thought it was clever or to purposely bug me, Paul always refused to use my preferred nickname in that slightly nasal voice of his. "Are you going somewhere after work?"

I didn't respond right away. Paul was harmless, sometimes a little pushy, but I hadn't had any kind of attention in a while and wasn't above admitting to myself his flirting stroked my ego. That didn't mean I wanted to lead him on, though. No way was I attracted to him. Not that there was anything wrong with him, he just wasn't my type. Okay, so I was being shallow that the 5'9", skinny except for a soft pot belly, thinning hair and deep set brown eyed 35-year-old always smelled like too much garlic for my liking. We were friends as far as I was concerned, and always did my best to deflect his playful advances without hurting his feelings. "You're so sweet." He winked in response to that. "You know me. I'm just heading home after." Because I didn't have a life. Trying not to depress myself, I shrugged.

Paul made an unhappy face at the shirt draped over my chair. "Still running his errands?"

We'd had this talk with rather alarming frequency and though I usually felt vindicated discussing my ex with my coworker, I just didn't feel like getting into it. "Just doing a favor on my lunch."

Paul snorted, the soft roundness of his cheeks puffing out as he exhaled through widened nostrils. "You are way too kind to him after what he did to you." I'd poured out my heart far too many times to complain that Paul had his own opinion on the subject. "I mean seriously, couldn't he have waited at least a year before marrying again?" Nothing new in that question, though it still stirred bubbling resentment. "You should toss his shirt in the trash."

I had to admit I was shocked and half loving the idea, the image making me giggle.

Paul grinned back, visibly feeding off my approval. As I sank into my seat with a sigh, wishing I could just trash the last ten years or so and start again, Paul stood, joining me, moving into my cubicle and leaning over the desk.

There were only a few times he managed to make me uncomfortable, and all of them involved me trapped in my chair with him leaning over me, one hand on the back, the other on my desk, creating too personal of a space that I couldn't avoid or escape while the permeating scent of garlic made my throat tighten.

I watched his pupils dilate, his tongue sweep over his lips and felt panic churn. Please, don't let him ask me out. I didn't want to lose the one friend I had in the office by saying no outright. And dating him was totally out of the question. My heart fluttered anxiously, pattering against my ribs, the slow motion sensation of dread dragging at me as if trying to drown me in a long and horrible horror movie moment.

"Have you heard?" Phew, no request for a date. His tone of voice, half-whispered conspiracy making me lean in despite myself now that the pressure was off. "There's talk of downsizing. Looks like two or three positions are going to be eliminated."

Yikes, that would suck for the new hires.

Since I'd been here twenty years, I knew I was safe from the axe, but it had to be tough being young and fresh to a new job only to find out the economy meant things didn't work out.

"Any idea who's going?" I glanced around the office, keeping my own voice down as Paul shrugged.

"Not yet," he said, winking. "But assessments are being done, just a heads up." He leaned closer. "You're welcome."

Wait, did I need to be worried? A faint touch of panic woke, fluttered bird-like in my chest. But before I could ask him if he thought so, a strident and familiar voice cracked like the proverbial whip I was certain she kept in her office, startling us both and catching our attention.

"Good morning, everyone." Judy Carpenter's greeting was met with murmurs from the rest of the staff in the large, cubicle filled office. I watched her stare at Paul, our boss's stern expression chasing him back to his own seat where he glared back at her like she'd offended him. I'd always liked Judy, but today, I felt a little nervous. I really had to make sure I did my best to shine the next little while, just in case.

Meanwhile, Judy smiled, a quick and firm expression that resembled an attempt at looking friendly rather than a genuine go of it. I paid dutiful attention while she waited for the rest of the whispering to die down, giving her my focus. She'd earned it, after all, taking me on as her assistant after college twenty years ago. I'd been here just a few months less than her, though I'd stayed in my position while she'd risen the ranks, now the managing partner. Maybe it should have bothered me I'd never really gone any further than desk jockey. Not that there was much personal growth to be had at Sawyer, Lee and Carpenter Architectural. Sure, I could have pursued somewhere else that would give me options, but I liked Judy. So many people were unhappy with their jobs, right? I had a great boss, strong, fair, consistent. What more could I ask for? And while I admit I could do this job with my eyes closed, it gave me time to work on my book, so I forgave myself. All of my nervousness about the possibility of losing my job went away. I had too much seniority, right?

And, I reminded my whispering ego while Judy turned toward her office door and the person emerging behind her, this was a well-paying job I couldn't really afford to lose, boring an pedestrian or not. How many divorced women were in the kind of position I had? I was damned lucky and that was that.

My mental chatter came to an abrupt halt when the tall, broad-shouldered man Judy stepped aside for came to a halt and nodded to all of us, hands on his hips. Vibrant green eyes caught and held mine a moment as his gaze swept the room, his smile, at least, real, authentic, flashing white teeth in the kind of face that men's magazine covers are made of.

I held my breath, only realizing I had when I was forced to take in fresh oxygen or keel over. Meanwhile, Mr. Delicious in his white cotton t-shirt that hugged his well-defined chest in ways I thought I would die to hug nodded to Judy, still smiling, showing the kind of perfect profile, strong jaw, straight nose, wavy dark hair, muscular neck, that had me wishing I wasn't just hugging him.

Damn, I wanted to be that t-shirt.

Judy was tall, near 5'10", especially in heels, but he had inches on her. I fought not to drool as Judy spoke again.

"Thank you for your attention, everyone." I didn't miss the soft tittering laughter from two of the junior assistants on the other side of the room. Right, so my eyes weren't deceiving me and no, Captain Yummypants wasn't a figure of my imagination. Even Judy seemed acutely aware of the scrumptious feast standing next to her, smiling more like a regular person than her typical stoic stiffness. "This is Elliot Parker." Handsome waved, a casual gesture that tugged the tight t-shirt over his chest in suggestive ways. No, wait. That was my imagination. Seriously, I had to get a grip on my hormones. "He is here to shoot the

Master's residence for City Central Magazine."

"Happy to be here." Okay, so someone that good looking? Couldn't have a voice like velvet, deep and warm as if he'd been doing voiceovers for Hollywood his entire life. Not fair. Next thing I'd find out he smelled amazing. Which meant, I found myself blushing, I'd have to get close to him to prove.

What was wrong with me?

"He's at our disposal for only a couple weeks," Judy said. Yes, she was talking, her lips were moving and sound was coming out. Why then did it take a moment to register what she actually told us? "So let's give him a big company welcome." More giggling from the corner. My cheeks were so hot I had to struggle not to fan myself while I frowned at their impropriety even as my mind wanted to make sure he got that welcome personally. "Whatever he wants, give it to him."

Oh my god, did Judy even know what she was saying right now? More laughter, this time from the bulk of the staff, mostly middle-aged women, though the men, Paul included, seemed sour about the reaction.

"Like we need a hotshot photographer around here, showing off." My cubical neighbor's grunting unhappiness came through loud and clear.

Meanwhile, the energy in the office had transformed from a lazy Sunday in the park to the North Pole at Christmas. Paul turned away, still scowling, while Judy continued her conversation with the handsome newcomer, leaving me to my own private thoughts.

Private naughty thoughts. The kind that would normally make me blush, but was feeding my inner author like nothing I'd ever encountered before. Buzzing even from this distance, I couldn't wait to get my hands on my computer and start writing. This man was sheer visual creative inspiration.

Smiling, I open my computer and, with a quick glance around to make sure no one was watching, started to write.

The raw tension rippling from the stranger's sudden appearance made Gabby gasp. How could he make her body quiver just at the sight of him? She wanted him now, with the physical need she'd only imagined possible, a quickening in her that would not be denied, feeding newfound willfulness she'd never possessed before.

Her approach to the bar felt effortless, carrying her hungry body into the danger zone, within his reach. She leaned over at the bar—

I paused suddenly, biting my lower lip. I always struggled with just throwing ideas down, needing to know where the story was going, sorting out the characters in my head. Funny, it seemed to come more quickly than usual, unfolding like it was meant to be.

Waitress. Customer who just walked in on a quiet night in a small town where everyone knew everyone and a stranger stood out, especially one like him. I glanced at Judy's office door where Elliot lingered before returning to my story.

"Would you like a drink, stranger?" She didn't mean to taunt him with her words. It was just a question, one she'd asked a million times, it seemed. But there was tension in her voice, a depth of sultry seduction she couldn't contain, inviting him closer and not just for a shot of whiskey.

He approached the bar, cowboy boots striking the floor in heavy thuds, face dark and expressionless, six-shooter low on one lean hip. His rippling biceps flexed as he reached for the shot glass, thick fingers engulfing the glass, sliding over the smooth surface, eyes never leaving hers. She found herself breathless, caught in his slow and deliberate motions, held captive by the long and suggestive trip the drink took from the bar to his parted lips.

Gabby's breath caught, her own lips damp, lower caught between her teeth. And not just the lips he could see, but those she hid beneath the heavy folds of her layered skirt. Lips he might get to taste if he played his cards right.

The shot glass hit the bar with a sound like

a gunshot, a tiny grin pulling at his full mouth, lighting his intensely green eyes. And, in that moment, as he finally looked her up and down in the devouring way she'd seen before but never felt so deeply in her life, she knew her reaction was matched by his.

She couldn't stand it. How long had it been since she'd taken a man to her bed? Too long, far too long, and from this gorgeous stranger's expression, he was as sex starved as she was, that bulge in his tight pants needing attention.

Gabby circled the bar, eyes locked on him, knowing her strutting walk was a challenge as much as an offer, the heat between her thighs driving her, unwilling to release her without his assistance. The need to quench the lust she'd suppressed for too long won as she gave in completely. He watched, silent but with his own naked wanting burning in his gaze as she stopped one stool from him and straddled it, grinding her pelvis against the rounded wooden edge, eyes locking on the straining bulge of his huge coc...

"I need this doc corrected." The file folder hit my desk with a thud as I jerked out of Gabby's head and back into the office. The scowling blonde standing over me didn't seem to notice I wasn't actually working, not even glancing at my screen, just glaring like she always did. I gaped at Lauren Spalding instead of answering, my body's response to what I'd been writing—living, breathing, experiencing as I wrote it—fought against my need to hide what I'd been up to behind a huge flush of embarrassment. "I need it done this afternoon so I can finish my proposal by end of the day."

I glanced down at the three-inch-thick file and back up at my frustrated coworker, finally finding my own irritation. I had no idea if she knew I called her bitch face in my head or if Paul was the one who drew the rude pictures about her that appeared magically next to the coffee machine. Didn't matter, not when she was always foisting off her work on me.

I usually just let her bully me. It was easier than arguing. But not this time. Nope, I had Gabby's excess sexuality burning a hole in my underwear and last night's adventure giving me more spine than I was used to. I registered the shock in Lauren's face, knowing it matched my own despite my inability to stop myself, as I slammed my laptop closed so violently she backed off.

"I've done my part of this proposal," I said, offering the file back to her.

Whatever ground I'd gained with her, I lost it as her face tightened. Pissed me off she was so beautiful and despite only being here five years was already at the same level as me. No, I wasn't above jealousy.

"Please." She managed to ask instead of

ordering despite the fact I didn't work for her so maybe I had made an impression. "Just get it done and no more fuck ups." She turned and stormed away toward her desk, leaving me to scowl after her.

What did she mean? I worked hard on this proposal, recognizing the Marigold file immediately. I'd been meticulous, knew my job well enough I wasn't about to make any mistakes. And she was blaming me if something wasn't right? We'd just see about that.

I sank into my office chair in a huff, flipping open the cover of the file while mixed emotions ate away at my insides. I hated being interrupted while I was on a roll, when I was in writing flow. Worse, I had to admit, because my body still tingled from the imaginary sex Gabby was about to have with the gorgeous stranger.

Right then, work it was. I'd channel my frustration into whatever it was Lauren thought I'd done. It wasn't until I flipped to the accounting pages, charting the funding proposal for the multi-million dollar mansion build I realized we had a problem. And that it wasn't mine.

This mess? It had Paul's name all over it. So why then did Lauren think it was me?

CHAPTER SEVEN

Tigen, Brewer and Donaldson had ten floors midway up the Carousel, the newest high rise in the city and about as far from my office as going home. I always felt a little intimidated when I had to go inside. Or was that a lot intimidated? Smack dab in the center of financial, legal and business central, coming down here reminded me I'd been in the same office, at the same desk, for far longer than I'd ever intended to.

Richard, on the other hand, made sure he'd risen in the ranks as often as possible and wasn't above lording that over me. As I stood at the elevator doors, the marble and icy glass of the ultra-modern lobby making me wish I'd brought more than just my sweater, it suddenly felt as if he was already looking down at me from his office on the twenty-third floor. Why did his shirts suddenly feel so heavy lying across my arm? And why did it seem like the others waiting for the doors to open, to carry us up into the belly of the beast, knew why I was there?

I shifted where I stood, uncomfortable, neck warm, cheeks heating while I fought against my rising questions. Was Jones right? Was this codependent behavior? I shuffled onto the elevator and kept my head down, not wanting to draw attention to the fact I was frowning and fighting an internal battle I knew I'd never win. Not fair of her to make me doubt like this. I had my relationship with my ex-husband sorted out. This was none of her business. As the bell rang and jerked me out of my spinning thoughts, I stepped out into the bright, polished foyer of Richard's law firm with a visible shake of my head. Instead of letting further doubt hold me back, and rather than taking the smart, easy route that involved dropping off my delivery, I instead chose to prove I knew what I was doing, if only to myself, and marched right past Richard secretary, Sheila.

That is, I tried to. "Excuse me, Mickey." Her smile never failed to make me feel small and I jerked to a halt, cheeks on fire yet again. "He's in the middle of something." That's right, Mickey. You're not important enough in Richard's secretary's eyes to warrant any kind of latitude. "I can take that for you."

There were times in the past I'd let Sheila bully me. Times I'd stepped aside, been the good girl, stayed quiet and let her have the victory she seemed to need over me. I was positive she'd been delighted that Richard left me, noted a subtle shift in her attitude after the divorce. Sheila's prim outer shell couldn't hide her contempt and disdain. I hated reacting to it, accepting it and today, of all days? That backbone I'd uncovered wasn't taking no for an answer.

I smiled, just enough, head up, shoulders back. Stopped Sheila right in her black heels and skirt suit. The startled look on her face could have been from that tight bun she was wearing, but I doubted it, felt buoyed by her reaction, smiling wider as I reached for the door handle to Richard's office. "He's expecting me." Before she could stop me, I pulled open the frosted glass and strode inside, feeling about as powerful as I ever had and ready for anything.

At least, that was what I told myself, until I had to actually face the man across the room. Richard sat in his dark leather lounger, looking like the king I knew he was, traces of silver at his temples, fine lines appearing around his dark eyes as he looked up, frowning at my interruption.

I needed to hate him for what he'd done to me. I wished I could bring myself to at least be angry. Instead, as always, I found myself melting a little, the fantasies I wrote about as much seated in my old love for him as the imaginary characters I built around what I'd always craved. Why did age just seem to make him all the more delicious to look at? Like a seasoned stallion instead of a fool hearted colt. Old desire stirred inside me, desire I quickly suppressed as his frown turned to a flash of understanding and then dismissal that hurt far more than it should have.

He went back to what he'd been reading, casually crossed legs facing me, sleeves rolled up far enough to show off his muscular forearms, the trace of a tan he'd acquired since I'd seen him last. I knew from experience he smelled amazing and hated that I lingered longer than necessary, hoping for a breath of that scent as a reminder of what I used to have.

"I brought your shirts." How freaking obvious, Mickey. And pathetic, truth be told. I cleared my throat as he closed over the file in his lap, setting it aside as he slowly rose to his six foot height. "What time are you in court?" That was better. Less servant and more caring friend.

Richard's slow smile wasn't helping the

melting feeling inside me and as he approached in that long-legged stride so familiar it made me ache a little I forgave him his initial reaction to my arrival. "Sorry, Mick." His tenor voice had a comforting tone to it and I found myself smiling back, holding out his shirts. "Just needed a moment to finish reading. Thank you for this." He took the dry cleaning bag from me, draping it over the back of the chair that framed the small lounge at the front of his large office. I knew from previous visits he had a killer view, but I couldn't ever really seem to focus on the world outside when I was with Richard. How was it I could live in such hope for a smile, a hug, a caress when I knew better? Or even a, "Let's get out of here, I know a great hotel just around the corner."

I snapped back to the here and now when Richard's voice interrupted old wounds being torn wide all over again. "You're so sweet to do this." One big hand settled on my arm a moment, squeezed, before falling away. "Turns out my court date's been postponed, so I didn't need the shirt until tomorrow after all."

Which meant I gave up my lunch to deliver something he didn't even need. Except when he leaned in and kissed my cheek, lips barely brushing my skin as that scent of him I still dreamed about filled me with emotions I fought to contain, it was all worth it.

"I really do appreciate it." He'd perfected

that all-encompassing smile, that grin that made me believe I was the only one in the world, the only one that mattered. He'd won cases with that warm and engaging expression, that Hollywood shine. I was so lost in it I failed to realize until I found myself on the other side of his glass door he'd escorted me out without me knowing I'd been moving. His hand at the small of my back distracted enough I don't have time to think of something to say, to make an excuse to linger. He gestured to Sheila who rose to join him as he winked at me.

"Thanks again, Mick. See you Sunday." Shelia brushed past me, pulling the door firmly closed behind her, blocking me out and leaving me cold and aching and wondering what I was even doing there.

Regret and Richard went hand in hand. As I turned toward the exit, the elevators and the long ride back to the office, I argued my choices and my attachment to the man who left me for another woman. We still cared for each other, that much was obvious. I secretly stuck my tongue out at the judgmental woman in my head. Childish, yes, but I was tired of doubting myself. Wasn't that a part of what Jones wanted for me? To be decisive?

I needed to get back to work, to get to that mess of a file. Because my feelings for Richard? Yeah, those weren't going anywhere.

CHAPTER EIGHT

I made it back to the office in just under the hour I had for lunch, telling myself I wasn't really hungry despite the soft rumbling in my stomach. A strong cup of coffee with lots of cream and sugar took the edge off while I settled in to deconstruct and rebuild the file Lauren handed me.

Not my job, but whatever. I knew from experience if I'd tried to get Paul to fix his mistakes it would only make things worse. He liked working on his own projects rather than helping with others, so it was never worth it to stir that particular pot. Instead, knowing it meant I'd be here after hours but without much of a choice, I accessed the file in the database and began to correct the funding estimates for the project.

It was easier to do so when I tapped into pride in my work. I'd been handling financial management for new builds for years and wondered why Paul had even been asked to take this one on. Honestly, Lauren should have come to me originally. But wait. She'd blamed me for the mess in the first place. I made a note to check in with her and confirm I hadn't been on the file. She really needed to check her workflow history.

One cup of coffee later and I was up and looking for more. The empty pot with the black crust burned to the bottom was just another piece in the frustration of my day. I rinsed it clean, sighing over the slow drip of the machine, studying the sheet of figures in my hand, noting only in passing that someone else had entered the break room and joined me by the percolating stuff of life.

"Just what I was hoping for." My head snapped up at the sound of that deep voice, the smile on the other end of it making my stomach flip over. As Elliot's green eyes met mine, I felt a tiny voice squeak in my head, a voice that whispered, "Richard who?"

I stared at the handsome photographer, shocked to discover he was even more attractive close up. Shocked, actually, to find him standing two feet from me, looming over me in his casual button up and jeans that hugged him in the kind of delicious embrace I wished suddenly was mirrored by his arms around me.

It was clear he was waiting for me to say something but I couldn't even stammer a single word, so surprised by this physical reaction to him I almost ran. I'd never felt attracted to anyone but Richard and that need for my ex? Paled in sudden comparison to the surge of visceral want that swept through me while Elliot's smile deepened as if he knew what I was thinking about him. Naughty, naughty thoughts I couldn't control.

My silly palms were sweaty all of a sudden, the pages in my hand fluttering slightly as he closed the distance, never breaking our gaze.

"Hi," he said like I wasn't the most awkwardly uncomfortable person he'd ever met. "I'm Elliot."

I just stared at him, loving the slight dimple on his chin and how there was gold in his green eyes, adding an almost metallic glitter. His smile widened while I finally managed to swallow and stick out one hand, the one clutching a pen that made it impossible for him to shake. Blushing all over again, I stammered an apology while he laughed, liberated it with his left and shook my now free one.

His skin was warm, firm, the hands of a

man who didn't mind working hard. Nothing like Richard's softly manicured grip far too tight for comfort sometimes. Elliot's handshake felt genuine, engulfing but without aggression. And was it me or did his touch linger a moment before he let me go, replacing my pen in my limp fingers?

"And your name is?" He laughed again, leaning one hip against the counter while I fought for a breath and the ability to speak.

"I'm, um, Mickey." I almost tried to shake his hand again, caught myself and giggled. Please, let it not have made me sound like a total airhead. "Michaela O'Keefe." Like I needed the reminder at the moment I'd kept Richard's last name. It suddenly felt fake, as if I hadn't taken the last step I needed to move on.

Elliot nodded in response, still smiling that sexy smile that reminded me of the heat I'd felt kindled last night at the sex party. That same heat I'd been writing about thanks to his appearance this morning. And then I was blushing harder because surely he could see it written all over my face, this attraction I had for him?

"Nice to meet you, Mickey." He gestured at the coffee pot. "Mind if I steal a cup?"

I shook my head, breathless, still not sure what to do with myself, my hands, the papers and pen seemingly in the way and yet held like shields between me and the gorgeous beast standing so close to me. I'd always had issues with handsome men, felt uncomfortable and out of place around them. Ever since my first teen crush humiliated me in public, I'd carried this worry that every handsome guy I met was waiting to repeat the performance. Part of the reason I clung to Richard. Yes, I'd worked that much out in therapy, thanks.

"Thank you." Elliot reached across the front of the machine, arm brushing my hip as he helped himself to a mug. I almost moved out of the way but found myself holding still, enjoying this little moment of delightful excitement. I could use this later when I revisited Gabby's encounter with the gunslinger. Research, right? Just research.

Elliot spoke again and I almost missed what he's saying I was so wrapped up in the sound of his voice. It was the kind of rumbling tone that would make Zeus jealous, all baritone and sexy. He could get a job as a voice-over artist in the movies, no problem.

And then I registered what he was saying and I gaped at him, all of the stirring heat lost when I realized what he'd said. "Sorry, what?"

He laughed, easy and warm. "I don't mean to be so forward, but if you have time before I go, I would love to shoot you." He winked. The most adorably hot wink I'd ever seen let alone been the recipient of. In fact, I was pretty sure that wink was his superpower.

Half-giggling, half-snorting I shyly gave him a meager wave that reminded me of a broken wing flopping ineffectually before I ran. Literally *ran* back to my desk.

Without my coffee or, I realized with horror, saying yes or no to his proposal. And while it was likely said proposal had been totally misconstrued in my clearly hormone-influenced mind, the idea he wanted to take my photos for reasons that had nothing to do with just taking my photos wouldn't leave me.

I needed to talk to Jones. Hell, I needed Jones to talk for me.

I slipped back into my haven of a desk and cubicle, smiling openly, thinking about what just happened. No way was I going back in the break room for coffee, not until he left. I just couldn't go in there and increase the awkward disjointedness of my departure by returning and admitting I'd been so overwhelmed by the offer I'd reacted like a thirteen-year-old girl with a crush. Then again, I had reacted that way and damn if I wasn't feeling just like I had the afternoon Tommy Sharpel told the entire school he wasn't interested in me and to leave him alone already.

But even my usual lingering doubts couldn't crush the fact Elliot said he wanted to shoot me. Yes, I'd blossomed from the gangly redhead with the knobby knees and too many freckles into an attractive woman. I was aware of my appearance, that I could even pass for beautiful with the right clothes and makeup. But never in a million years would I ever have dreamed someone like Elliot would want to take my photos.

Which meant he did have an agenda. I chewed my bottom lip, staring at the screen in front of me without seeing the numbers there, catching his departure from the break room out of the corner of my eye. I caught my breath, doing my best not to stare as he strode with that confident stride, one big hand cradling his mug, smiling at those he passed like he belonged here. My mind froze until he disappeared behind Judy's door and then started up all over again.

Could it be he saw in me something he liked? And all of a sudden I couldn't help but feel good about myself. A strange but delightful lightheadedness came over me, my body flooded with whatever biochemical triggered euphoria. I even started humming to myself and, rather than tackle Lauren's file, instead opened my laptop to continue the saga of Gabby and her gunslinger.

"You don't have it done yet?" Speak of the she-devil. Lauren had somehow approached silently, and I actually jerked in shock when she spoke, squeaking out a little meep of surprise at her appearance. She looked about as happy to be standing there as I was to have her hovering. "Seriously, Mickey, what have you been doing all morning? I told you it was a priority." Paul snorted behind me and I knew if I needed to commiserate after he'd be all over it. Except, he was the reason I was in this spot in the first place. I couldn't win. "I need the quote ready before the end of the day and I mean the end of the day."

I stuttered something, the happy state of things vanishing as bitterness and guilt took the place of delight. Lauren didn't wait for me to answer, instead storming off toward Judy's office. The immediate hit of defeat weighed on my shoulders, my hands releasing my laptop back into the bag as I glared in anger at the screen. I just knew Paul was watching, waiting for me to turn around and comment about Lauren. We'd shared enough snarky backbiting over her ambition over the last year or so it would have been easy. This time, instead of stalling, I dove back into the file and did his job.

The good part was the mistakes were easy to fix with the right amount of information. The bad part, that research, the vital part of the file, would take the rest of the day. A total bummer, considering all I really wanted to do was write. No, it wasn't lost on me I was at work and meant to be working since that was what they were paying me for. But Paul's mistake and Lauren's attitude were making my already rather dull job an actual chore.

Well, there was always tonight after work. I could stop and grab a bottle of wine on my way home. Drink a glass or two to loosen up and then slide into Gabby's world.

I almost gasped as a shuddering surge grasped me and shook me in my seat at the thought of my character's pending affair with the gunslinger. A soft giggle escaped me while I waved my hand in front of my face, fanning my heated cheeks. I hadn't expected that physical reaction just from thinking about a scenario before and, with renewed excitement and a spur of energy to propel me on, I tackled the report with more vigor than I'd ever thought possible.

Four hours later, full speed had turned sluggish, my eyes feeling bruised from the strain of making sense of what I was putting back together. I glanced at the clock on the corner of my screen and, to my happy surprise, found that not only was I almost finished, it was only 4:45PM.

Fifteen minutes to spare? Hell yes. Paul and Lauren both owed me big time.

I hit send on the file five minutes later and waited for her receipt so I knew she'd taken possession on the other end. The yellow flag jumped into position, marking that she was reviewing what I'd done while I scowled at the offending color, willing it to turn green. Which it did a moment later, though without a note of thanks or even a hint of appreciation for everything I'd done for her.

Not that it mattered, because I was over it and needed to get out of here. All I could think about was Gabby and the gunslinger and the evening that lay ahead. Not even Laura's lack of anything resembling basic human decency could quash my joy at the thought of spending time writing, drinking and revisiting those very interesting and embarrassingly naughty feelings I blushed just thinking about.

I grabbed my sweater from the back of my chair, laptop bag swung over my shoulder. Paul grinned as he rose and I knew from the way he looked at me was about to broach a drink offer, but I was already moving, waving at him farewell so I didn't have to come up with an excuse.

Turned out, I didn't need one. I wasn't even at the elevator when my phone chimed. Just glancing at the screen at the author of the text made me collapse inwardly and I suddenly wished I'd ignored my phone just this once.

It's Mom, Michaela. Like I didn't know that from her number. *Dinner tonight, 6 PM sharp.* We weren't scheduled for dinner tonight. Or were we? Maybe I'd forgotten on purpose to give myself a brief respite from the impending doom that was dinner with my family. *Don't be late, and no excuses.* Only she would end such a bullying text with an adorable smiley face.

CHAPTER NINE

The pot roast tasted stale and tough in my mouth as I listened to the endless rambling of Violet Gardener, victim, bully, mother.

"Richard is just like the rest of them, Michaela." It would have been funny if the conversation weren't so familiar, so utterly life-draining in its repetitiousness, a litany of complaints and accusations and whispered innuendoes I'd been listening to in one variation or another my entire life. "They're all cheaters. Just look at your father." Mom chewed a piece of her roast a moment before talking around it, the dark red lipstick she wore bleeding into the smoker's lines around her mouth. She'd gotten her hair done today from the perfect look of her carefully styled do, though the tight dress and excessive makeup was a bit much for a weeknight dinner with her two daughters. Well, one daughter at the moment. Just like my sister, Tara, to be able to dodge Mom's unhappiness while I was forced to suffer.

The sharpened ovals of my mother's matching red pointed fingernails could have stabbed someone to death if she'd made the attempt. Speaking of which. Please, just kill me and put me out of my misery. "I couldn't trust him for five seconds." Oh right, she was still talking about Dad. I stared down at my plate in the dim light of the chandelier overhead, the china holding the bulk of my dinner I just couldn't choke down, the dark burgundy napkin a great thing to hang onto. Like a lifeline in my lap. "On the night you got sick with the measles, he was running around with our neighbor." I glanced sideways at the empty seat where my absent sister should have been sitting. Unlike me, Tara never seemed to mind listening, though I often wondered at these travesty of family bonding dinners if she heard a word Mom said or if she was lost in her own thoughts. Tara was always better at blocking Mom out than I was.

"The gall of that man, walking out like that while you were sick." My mother's chewing became more aggressive, jiggling the wattles of her heavy jawline. She'd recently lost a large amount of weight and preened over the fact. "And there I was, left alone to take care of you and your sister. Your father abandoned us for some *booty*." Inhale, Mick. Exhale. "Richard is just like him, you know. You married your father." She stabbed the air between us with her fork. "I knew from the start he was a womanizer. I never told you that he actually touched my arm and suggested something *inappropriate* during your rehearsal dinner." Actually, she had told me, many times before, though she'd never come out and said what this so called inappropriate comment might have been. "I was so shocked, though I have to say flattered, but so shocked I just let it go." Likely because it never happened. Bitterness tasted like Mom's pot roast.

"You are so much better off without him." Yes, Mother. "Though, you *do* need to get him to finally pay you what he owes you." I'd talked to Richard about that. Our divorce settlement wasn't anything of Mom's business. I'd never told her I'd walked away with a small amount, without the heart to push for more against the powerhouse lawyer I'd married. Didn't matter. It was only money. "The least he could do is set you up. I mean, it's your right. Your father left us nothing." Ah, yes, this was the real reason she brought up money, to continue her diatribe against Dad. "He is a coward and a loser. I had to use your college tuition just to survive because he left us desolate." So desolate she managed two trips that year, one to Maui and the other to Paris to console herself. I remembered, all right.

Speaking up, acting out, would get me nowhere. Instead, I just sat and listened with my head down, trying not to absorb any of my mother's ramblings. I knew better than to challenge her or even bother to respond. The former would end in a catastrophic meltdown I'd pay for weeks into the future and the latter would be ignored. Mom didn't want a conversation. She wanted a silent witness.

The front door opened, the sound of footfalls coming toward us in a hurrying patter of heels that preceded Tara's arrival. Mom looked up, her harsh expression turning to a beaming smile as my younger sister hustled into the room. Her perfect little figure stood out in designer jeans and a fitted cropped jacket, her dark bob swinging around her chiseled cheeks I was positive her plastic surgeon husband had something to do with because Tara's nose and lips and eyes didn't always look like that. Neither did her rather impressive rack.

Bitterness transferred from Mom to sister in a heartbeat. Which meant my night was about to get even better.

Tara moved right to Mom, air kissing her cheeks, speaking instantly before Mom could take a breath. "Sorry I'm late, the kids had soccer and I, of course, am the only competent mother at their practice to make sure all the kids had their equipment. And the new uniform shirts, what a disaster." She tossed her hands in the air after setting her expensive handbag on the table, smiling and eye rolling at Mom. My mother patted her hand with an expression of sympathy while Tara turned her eyes to me. We couldn't have looked less like sisters, me with my tall body, wide shoulders, red hair and she with her dainty and petite good looks. I thought about Elliot and soured slightly, knowing if he met Tara she'd be the one he'd want to photograph. Everyone always said she was the prettiest. "How is the book coming along, Mick?" She threw that question at me just like she always did, fake interest making me wish I'd kept my mouth shut instead of, in a moment of weakness, trying to impress her or Mom with my decision to be a writer.

"It's a long process. I'm getting there." I hated those words, the defeat of that excuse I'd used one too many times. It made my blood boil to watch her little smirk of judgment flicker over her full lips. And made me even more determined, instead of less for once, to finish my book and prove her lack of faith wrong.

Of course our mother didn't even acknowledge Tara's tardiness. "Don't encourage her, Tara, dear. You know Michaela's daydreaming won't amount to much."

And that was the Gardener family at their very best.

"Now look at Bill." And she was back on her man rant, though she made a horribly sensual face when she talked about her newest and youngest toy. "You get them young and then you squeeze them into what you want them to be." Was I really sitting here listening to this? "I mean it's the only way to keep them on lead. Right, Tara?"

My sister poured herself a glass of wine, ignoring the food on the table as she sat back and sipped the dark red. Mom went on as if she hadn't asked my sister a question.

"You do a fantastic job with that husband of yours." My plastic surgeon brother-in-law was about as meek as a mouse and doted on Tara. "Bill is very well trained." Mom saluted my sister and the two clinked glasses.

I couldn't eat anything else. In fact, I felt like I was going to be sick. This conversation was, after all, a continual time loop I knew I'd be living for the rest of my life. My younger sister Tara had it all. A gorgeous husband that doted over her, two perfect kids, both straight-

A students, not to mention great at sports and musically inclined. The oldest, Hayden, barely twelve, wanted to be an astronaut, for god sake.

And Tara's house! I didn't dare get Mom started on that particular topic. A historic reno in the oldest part of the city, it was easily five thousand square feet, overlooking the river. They were friends with the governor, even got invites to their Thanksgiving dinner. Not to mention her skin was flawless. Not that I was comparing us or anything.

For the next hour, the conversation wound through complaints from Tara about an incompetent teacher that dared give her youngest, ten-year-old Ryden, an A minus on an assignment at that fancy private school he went to, back to Richard, naturally, and my father. I was sure tonight would be a typical repeat of every other family dinner, that it would end as it always did, with Mom reduced to fake tears over how we never appreciated her, drunk on her fourth glass of wine, while Tara made an excuse and left early, leaving me to make sure our mother didn't fall and hurt herself getting to bed.

A perfect night, right? Except, things were about to take on such epically perfect (hello sarcasm, my old friend) proportions I might as well have been having a blast at a theme park all evening.

Tara turned to me with an open smile, her eyes wide and innocent, as she dropped a bomb in my lap and waited for it to explode. "Michaela, did you hear? I was sure you'd be the one to tell me, not the other way around." She wrinkled her nose, tipping her glass in my direction. "How delightful for Richard and his new wife."

Mom's face creased in a frown while she looked back and forth between us and confusion made my stomach churn.

"Whatever are you talking about, Tara?" Mom slurred her words enough I knew she was on the edge of too much wine, but there was something about the way Tara watched me that made my heart pound, my chest tighten, my breath catch.

"Why, you don't know." Tara batted her eyes at me, a faint moue of disappointment meant to look, I guessed, like concern. "I guess he was waiting to tell you himself." She shrugged, sipped, smiled. "I'm sure you'll be happy for him, though. After all, it's a miracle, isn't it? The fact the two of them are having a baby?"

CHAPTER TEN

My mouth immediately went dry, pasty, every scrap of moisture sucked free. There was no way I heard Tara correctly, and yet her words still rang in my head, making it impossible to speak, to catch my breath.

"Richard and his new wife, what's her name again?" Tara seemed delighted she caught me off guard. I could see that Tara was talking and her words were making sounds but my brain's ability to process had shut off. Was this what it felt like to short-circuit? "Mickey, darling, please don't be difficult. What's her name?" Tara must have known she's delivered what feels like a death blow but didn't seem to care.

"Chere Summers." Chere with her sleek black hair and her bright blue eyes, her porcelain skin and petite frame that matched Tara's. They could have been sisters, leaving me out of this whole thing entirely. Wait, was that really my voice? Why did it sound so far away? "Pregnant?" I hadn't intended to add that plaintive word at the end of my response. It escaped my lips while my poor heart thudded a sympathetic beat or two before settling back into rhythm.

I stared at Tara, at Mom, begging them with all my being to stop the train wreck that threatened to crash into me at breakneck speed. Except, of course, they were both smiling and nodding, my nightmare complete.

"Oh yes, I think she's a couple of months in." Tara shrugged like it was no big deal while everything inside me that ever thought I might in fact be good enough, worthy of Richard and the life we'd shared together, burned to ash before collapsing to dust. "Can you imagine? Not even married for six months and they are starting a family." A family. Richard was starting a family. Without me. "And you, Mick." Tara's tone told me she was trying to be supportive though the careful way she watched me, almost eager in her observation, spoke louder than words, the sister I knew shining through. "They have no consideration at all for you and how you feel about it."

As Tara applied more gasoline onto the already tense moment, I couldn't even muster anger, not while my empty insides ached for the one thing Richard always told me he never wanted. The one thing I'd begged for and now, as if to spite me, that single thing he'd granted his new wife.

Numbness swept over me, the truth a blow that granted me some peace behind a wave of uncaring I dove into just to hide from the pain I knew would surface eventually. Best to let it shelter me, to pad me from my watchful mother, my spiteful sister, even as I was forced to sit there and listen to them chatter about the baby. The numbness spared me the details, though, the low hum of their words blurred, softened until I couldn't make out what they were saying specifically. I found myself rather casually lifting my glass of wine and downing it, tasting more like rotten fruit then the usual heavy naked Chardonnay my mother favored. But, at least I was safe in my bubble of numb, something I'm sure the two at the table found immensely disappointing.

Thing was, I had enough of this charade, long before Tara mentioned Chere's state of affairs. For the first time, though, with the blackout of my emotions giving me strength I usually didn't have, I pushed the elegant armchair across the hardwood with a startlingly loud squeal, catching their attention and silencing them. Mom's frown told me she disapproved of my manners. I stared at her as I stood, for once in my life not caring even a little bit what my mother thought.

I'm not sure what I said after that, only vaguely recalling thanking Mom for dinner, nodding to Tara, before taking my leave. Frankly, I was almost like a drunk, stumbling to the front door of Mom's apartment, turning the handle to escape what had become a dungeon of hell and finding myself in need, yet again, of air. At least the numbness lingered with me, still shielding me from what I could only guess would be an epic meltdown the moment I was alone.

Fine. I could handle that. I was a grown woman.

Uh-hum. I couldn't get to the subway quick enough. I barely remembered the walk, repeating a mantra in my head to keep myself together. Don't think about it. Don't think about it. Don't. Think. About. It.

It wasn't until I was sitting on the hard bench, the doors of the subway sliding closed next to me, I finally felt a traitor thought surface from beneath the black blanket keeping me safe. Richard was having a baby.

I shook my head, biting my lower lip as hard as I could, refusing to cry here, like this, over a future that would never be, a future he told me he didn't want. He was always so adamant that he didn't want kids. This had to be a mistake. Yes, exactly. Tara had to be lying, torturing me the way she always did.

Except, as I exited the subway at my stop, shoulders heavy, feet dragging, the ten minute walk ahead of me feeling like a long, lonely journey to the end of nowhere, I forced myself to accept the truth. Richard was having a baby. Without me.

I stumbled over a broken bit of sidewalk, catching myself at the last moment, shaking not from the fright of the near collapse but being forced to face the fact that not only were we through—yes, we were divorced, but I'd clung to hope, I admitted it now, in the dark, on the street, alone and vulnerable and very, very broken—but he had given the woman he'd chosen over me the only thing I'd ever really wanted.

A neon sign shone bright as the morning sun up ahead, catching my attention while I snuffled and wiped at my nose with the side of my hand, grateful I wasn't all-out crying just yet but knowing it was imminent. I needed to get home, safe behind the closed door of my apartment, to hide physically if I couldn't mentally and emotionally, from the onslaught of my pending meltdown. Except, as I stared at the sign, the name Tally's familiar, I instead caught my feet carrying me down the steps beneath street level and into the local 24-hour bar.

I'd never been there before and almost instantly regretted my decision that wasn't an actual decision but a reactionary act. But as I stood on the threshold, the heavy door swinging shut behind me, the dank air of the half-filled and rather dingy establishment washing over me, I let my usual nervousness about being alone in a place like this dissipate. I didn't have any alcohol in my apartment and, damn it, I needed a drink.

I took a moment to pick my route, glancing past the "L" shaped bar on the left to the small four seater tables that decorated the rest of the room. There was a gap at the bar, so I headed that way, keeping my eyes on the empty stool I planned to plant myself on, ignoring the young woman singing to her guitar on the main stage at the far end of the room, next to the jukebox. She wrapped a song as I sat, one of the drunken customers yelling a profanity, followed by laughter. It didn't seem to faze her as she launched into another tune while I could barely keep it together and I was anonymous.

The bartender, a handsome enough young man with a beard and a tight black t-shirt offered the barest smile as I nodded to him, purse clutched in my lap. I knew I don't fit in here, but I didn't care.

"What'll it be?" He paused and I stared,

pretty sure he wouldn't have the kind of wine I usually drank, mind stuttering over my choices, and settling, for some reason, on Gabby and her bar in the book I was writing.

"Whiskey and coke," I heard myself say. "Double. On ice."

He nodded, turned to pour, while my brain spluttered at me. I hadn't had whiskey in my life, let alone a double. What was I thinking? What would it do to me? Not to mention I wasn't much of a drinker to begin with, the soft buzz of the wine I'd drunk far too quickly at my mother's still hovering behind the numbness. And a double, for goodness sake. What, did I think I was in the movies? Then again, as the bartender set the tumbler in front of me and I offered a bill to pay, it sounded about right after my kind of day.

I did my best not to taste it, instead tossing it back in three gulps. It's a bit harsh but softens after a moment and I wave for another. He serves me without comment, taking my money, drifting away to handle another customer and I'm vaguely disappointed. Here I was, an attractive single woman at a bar, alone, shattered by misery, dulling my pain with alcohol. Didn't he have some kind of duty to talk to me, to make me feel better? Wasn't there some kind of bartender's code that said he had to pay attention and comfort me in my time of need?

I stared down into my second drink as the first began to hit my blood stream, dark amber liquid casting my reflection back at me as I tried to collect my thoughts. And found a surge of anger at last in the bottom of the glass.

Fuck you, Richard. I would have given you babies. You asshole. What was wrong with *my* uterus? Nothing, that was what. She worked just fine. I took another swig of the drink, realizing I was all out again. I looked up, the numbness of my heart's protection replaced by the buzz of alcohol racing through me, ready to order another. And another. I just wanted to drink until I passed out. That was a great idea, the best idea I'd ever had.

Something touched my back, pressure all of a sudden, startling and invasive. It took me a moment to register what was going on, to realize where the contact was coming from, and when I finally looked up, it was into dark eyes far too close to mine.

"Hey there, pretty lady." He was in a suit, tie loose, top button undone, smile not so much friendly as it was rather hungry. "Can I buy you a drink?"

I shook off his hand, the touch of a strange man the very last thing I wanted right now. I accepted that sober, level-headed me would likely have smiled sheepishly and begged off. Hell, wouldn't have been in this place to start with. But pissed off and half-drunk me? She was a whole different animal.

"Back off." I turned to the bartender as he was sliding another drink across the bar at me. The guy who'd touched me did as he was told, though his angry mutter of, "No need to be a bitch, I was just being friendly," wasn't endearing. At least he left me alone as I asked.

As for the new drink, the bartender waved off my money and pointed at a grinning stranger at the end of the bar who lifted his own drink and saluted.

"It's on him," the bartender said. Was that contempt in his eyes?

I shook my head at my new suitor, mouthing, "No thanks," pushing the drink off to the side to add emphasis to my rejection. Drunk or not, I was in an uncomfortable position and suddenly felt like prey, that every man in the bar saw me as an opportunity. Single drunk chick clearly in a terrible state of mind meant possible score. Well, no thanks, not me. Not tonight. Or any night.

I prepped myself to bolt, when a hand on my back stopped me, trapping me in place. There's enough force behind this new touch I'm actually nervous.

"You look like a movie star, sweetie." The first guy gave in easily enough, and end-of-the-bar guy didn't put up a fuss. But I could tell from the stare in this particular man's deep-set eyes he was much more persistent. Or maybe it was the gasp-worthy waft of liquor-heavy breath violating my air consumption.

I squirmed to free myself from his proximity. Time to go. Except, as I turned the stool to try to hop down and escape, he pinned me with both hands on the bar, his rather bulky build, and not in a lean and fit kind of way, trapping me in place.

Time for angry Mickey to do her thing. "Excuse me, sir. I'm good, thank you. I'd like to leave now." And, great, just great. When I needed her, actually could have used her help? She abandoned me like the faithless bitch she was.

"I haven't seen you in here before." He swayed but stayed put, grinning. I glanced at the bartender, expecting at least a bit of help, only to find him ignoring the situation. Wait, wasn't it his job to make sure I was safe? How disappointing. At least, I would have been disappointed if I didn't suddenly feel so anxious. "I like meeting new people. Especially pretty ones." He lifted one hand from the bar and tried to touch my hair. I aimed for the gap in his little trap but didn't move fast enough. "Let's be friends, beautiful."

I was in trouble and I put myself here. I needed to do something, even if it was just squeak out another denial. Reach for the glass of whiskey I'd been gifted, maybe, toss it in this guy's face. Anything, Mickey, do something. Except I felt frozen, desperate and pathetic, as the big, fragrant and drunk man in front of me leaned closer like he was going to get far more personal than I would ever be comfortable with.

CHAPTER ELEVEN

“**I** think you've had enough for tonight, mate.”

I wasn't expecting that deep voice to interrupt, and neither, it seemed, was the drunk about to assault me. His head whipped around and I stared in shock, my own mind muddied by the whiskey I'd drunk, as Elliot confronted my so-called suitor. Where had he come from all of a sudden? I blinked as he settled one big hand on Mr. Over-Eager's shoulder and steered him calmly and even kindly away from me with what looked like a casual touch.

The drunk staggered a little, wincing, and I wondered if appearances were deceiving. But

Elliot's firm smile never wavered and the man I'd once feared cast me a sullen look before slinking off toward a table in the corner.

Elliot, meanwhile, took a seat next to me and helped himself to the free glass of whiskey, grinning as if he found this whole scenario hilarious. But when he spoke again, there was so much genuine kindness in his voice I felt tears sting the corners of my eyes. "Are you okay?"

I couldn't handle him being nice to me right now. In fact, if he continued looking at me like that, with such sweet compassion, I was going to fall into a weeping puddle of goo. "I'm fine." Even in my more than tipsy state, I could hear clearly how that came across as defensive. Elliot didn't react badly, instead finishing the whiskey with a toss of his head and a nod.

"Good to know," he said. "Sorry to interfere. I know you're perfectly capable of taking care of yourself. Just doing a new friend a favor."

"What are you doing here?" God, I just needed him to go but I didn't want him to leave. Did he know I was torn between falling apart and this newfound thrill of physical reaction I felt when he showed up? It was building inside me even now, the warmth between my legs, the fluttering of my heart as the night's events began to fall away, leaving only his smile, his green eyes with those reflective bits of gold, the scent of him as he leaned closer to answer. Honestly, what was wrong with me? Then again, I'd come to this bar to drink and forget. Maybe this option was better.

Elliot spoke as I juggled my heart and my wakened libido. "My hotel is just around the corner." Which meant he was just around the corner from my apartment. Why did that idea thrill me? "I like this part of the city." He stretched out his long legs toward me, leaning closer, but with a casual familiarity, not a come on. His big hands folded on the bar in front of him and I found myself moving closer as he went on, his smile lingering. "There's so many cool places and people to photograph." One eyebrow arched, head tilting slightly. "And you?"

"I live a block from here." And then I was blushing, though from the alcohol or the way his pupils dilated I wasn't sure. Or did I imagine that reaction from him? I really was far too drunk for my own good. "You call this part of the city interesting." I almost laughed, felt the need choking me, and not out of humor but sudden despair. "I call it a prison. I'm stuck here because my ex-husband cheated on me with a younger woman. A woman he married less than six months ago. And now their having a baby. My baby. The one I wanted." I found myself blubbering suddenly, gushing out the words in a rush that hurt my throat and my chest like I birthed something myself, a dark knot of anger and hurt that burned all the way out. I should have been embarrassed, ashamed. Instead, I stared into those kind, quiet eyes and poured out my heart. "I'm thirty-seven years old. I wanted children, begged him for them." Pathetic, I was so pathetic, still clinging to Richard and hope all this time only to discover he never really wanted me, did he? "What's wrong with me? I would have been a great mom." I took a breath, another, shocked I wasn't sobbing, that I was coherent. And that Elliot continued to listen, silent, watchful, without a hint of pity.

It freed me, so much so I let him have it all. "My whole world is falling apart. My job is eating me alive, I'm so bored. I haven't felt stimulated," I leaned a bit closer, whispering the confession, "and I mean *stimulated*, in a very long time. If ever." His eyebrows twitch, but that's his only reaction. Shock or judgment? Whatever, I'm almost done. Maybe. "I'm thinking it's a thing, you know? This pending meltdown. That women that haven't orgasmed in a very long time, or ever, can literally blow a gasket." Yes, exactly. That's what was happening to me right now. I was losing it. "When it happens, all hell breaks loose. I'll be the one on the six o-clock news, the big headline of the day." I snorted a laugh that's half-amused, half-resigned. "'Rejected

Single Female Runs Amuck in Toy Department.' It'll be the perfect ending, the perfect humiliation. Parents shielding their kids in fear of the lone lunatic throwing stuffed unicorns at the mothers as they walk by with their children."

Elliot laughed, soft, low, so sexy I felt my body shudder. Was he laughing at me? No, he got the joke, didn't he? Made bold by his reaction, I grabbed the front of his jacket, oblivious to the others in the room now, my whole world those green-gold eyes. "Did you know I had to go to a sex party to even know what a vibrator was? And yes, damn it, I bought one." Elliot's grin widened. "My bestie Jones had to drag me out of my apartment for me to even go." It suddenly struck me I sounded like a crazy person, my life dumped out in his lap in haphazard chunks of confession. Didn't stop me, though. "You'd like Jones." Of course he would. "Everyone does." I wished suddenly she was here. She'd tell me how to handle Richard and his pending fatherhood. Likely with a well-placed rock through the windshield of his Audi. "And the toys to choose from, the sales lady whips out this huge..." I demonstrated with my hands, though I was pretty sure I had the measurement wrong. Elliot laughed again, shook his head, but didn't comment. My eyes felt as wide as saucers, my voice dropping in volume and a little steam. "I mean, I write bloody romance novels." His pleased reaction made me backtrack. "Well, I'm working on my first book. But you would think I would know what I'm talking about." How the hell did I ever expect to write my book when I knew so little? I sagged against the counter, my purse still clutched against my stomach. "The well is all dried up and I'm dehydrated. Can't everyone see I'm in desperate need of refreshment?" That sounded corny even to me and I was drunk. Didn't stop me from going on, though. "I'm a shell, a clam really, not even a very interesting husk." I liked that analogy. I'd have to use it maybe. Except, of course, for the exceptionally pathetic truth behind it. "No one will ever want to be with a shell, will they? I'm going to be alone for the rest of my life." I finally looked away, tears returning. "My mother says so and she's always right."

Silence at last. And a gap in which embarrassment could finally grow. Except Elliot's hand reached out and took mine, freeing it from my death-grasp on the side of my purse, gentle, squeezing ever so slightly. "How long have you been a writer?"

I stared up at him again, but in open bafflement this time. "That's what you're asking me about? Being a writer? Did you hear a word I said?"

I immediately regretted my tone, the attack.

He didn't deserve that. He'd been nothing but kind. Elliot continued to be, reacting with a nod instead of anger. "I can see a lot of me in you," he said, low and soft, compassion making things worse. "I lived my own version of your story, Mickey, woke up from it finally a few years ago. I had something happen, an awakening, helped me get my head on straight." I held my breath, not sure what to say. "I promised myself if I ever got the chance, I'd pay what I learned forward with someone who needed it as much as I did."

Why was I so afraid of him in that moment? Like he'd threatened me instead of offering help, kindness, more of his sweet empathy. I lurched to my feet, hand pulling free of him, purse between us like a shield. "Thanks for the rescue earlier." He held still, watching me. Was that sorrow in his eyes? I was too drunk to accept it, too hurt. "And for listening to me ramble." There, that fixed it. "I'm okay, I just need to go home. It's just life, you know? I'm drunk, that's all." I bumped into a chair as I backed away from him, retreating. It was rude and horrible, a terrible way to treat someone who was so kind to me, but I had to go, had to breathe again.

What had my life become that I struggled for air so very often?

I spun and ran for the exit, making it without falling or running into anyone, knowing I was likely staggering a bit but not caring. One look back caught Elliot watching me go, that same kind expression on his face while my chest ached with longing to go back, to let him hug me and maybe even cry on his shoulder this time while my bitter mind drove me out the door and into the night.

CHAPTER TWELVE

I fumbled with my keys, leaning against my door, while the opposite one opened, shining light into my eyes from my neighbor's apartment.

"Postman delivered this to the wrong door." Mrs. Barrow always sounded like an old, cackling witch to me. Too much scotch—look who was talking, at least tonight—and cigarettes were layered in that voice. She handed over the inconvenience like she had company and it was a terrible waste of her time to do me a favor. "You have someone over? It was awful loud the other night around 7 PM. All that laughing and carrying on." Nosy neighbors were just the best and I wasn't exactly in the mood to deal with her right now, feeling the remains of the whiskey whispering to me to tell her where she could shove her attitude. While mine was in fine form. "You just be respectful of others, missy. Or I'll call the landlord."

She didn't wait for a reply, retreating back into her dwelling, still mumbling about youngsters and our missing respect for our elders, not to mention our lack of work ethic. I stood there, the door jam holding me up, as she slammed her door behind her, one hand heavy with the package, the other still fumbling my key.

This time, though, the shaking in my hand wasn't from the alcohol consumption. Nope, it came from awareness, acute and painful. I knew right away what was in the plainly wrapped brown paper package.

I set it on my small kitchen table, dropping my keys and purse in a chair before grabbing a knife from the drawer beside the sink. I was sure if anyone had been there to watch they'd have thought I was marching into battle, the knife's handle firmly grasped in one fist, my face likely grim and determined while I maneuvered the narrow distance between the counter and the table. I almost stopped myself from attacking the tape with the blade, buyer's remorse lingering. But, I still had enough whiskey inside me, not to mention the dull ache I felt left over from my encounter with Elliot, to move my hand of its own accord.

A moment later, a huge pink penis stared accusingly up at me from its home inside the box. Wait a second, this wasn't what I ordered. I'd wanted the cute, soft blue one, with the rabbit. No, wait, the dolphin. Right? Instead, I had in my possession a replica of the dildo Pam had used to demonstrate her hand job.

Well, if she could handle it, I could handle it. At least, the whiskey thought so. Now what? I needed batteries or something, right? I reached tentatively out to touch it, the knife slipping from my hand at the same moment, making me jump. When I did, I bumped the box, sending the whole thing tumbling to the floor.

Horror kicked in, the knife next to what looked like the dismembered penis of an oddly florescent man I'd just severed and abandoned on the tile in my kitchen. What the hell was I going to do with *that*? Had I ever seen one so big? Richard seemed rather wanting in comparison. That made me giggle. I felt my courage bolster as I stared at it, lying there, so ineffectual and yet challenging me to do something. For some reason the compulsion to check the front door took me over and I caught myself peeking to be sure I was alone. Because I hadn't lived alone since I found out Richard was cheating, silly girl.

With a deep breath and more courage than I thought I had in me, I bent quickly and grasped the soft silicone dildo in my hand, the other firmly gripping the back of a chair to make sure I didn't fall over. Dizzy from the alcohol and nerves, I wavered a bit on the way up, breath coming a bit fast. The first thing I noticed was the texture, soft but firm underneath, the bright pink startling against my own skin, the suction cup on the bottom wider than the neat little scrotum the designer thought was a good idea to tag onto this truly large fake penis.

God, there were actually massive veins running the length of the thing, with a grotesque head marked with a slit at the top. I'd given Richard enough blow jobs over the course of our marriage it looked far too much like the real thing while being out of this world at the same time. It slipped a bit and I catch myself rubbing my hand down the shaft before tentatively stroking it like the sales lady did the other night.

For the first time I noticed there was a cord attached to the bottom of the apparatus, dangling free. I missed seeing it on my first shock. At the end, a simple pink controller. This at least was safe to examine, the three buttons clearly marked. One for speed, one for power and the third for settings.

A single, daring thought crossed my mind

as I stared at the buttons, the memory of green and gold flashing in my mind. The ache was still there, the need he woke. I could use this while thinking about Elliot.

Just the prospect gave me a mix of chills and excitement I wasn't expecting. Naughty thoughts woke, feelings I hadn't planned on. Was this what being turned on felt like? Mixed with utter embarrassment?

I caught myself in a forced casual walk toward my bedroom like I was at a dinner party and I didn't want anyone to know I was drunk. Was I really considering this? Yes, yes, I was. I'd bought the damned thing and there was no time like the present.

My bedroom door closed with a soft snick and I stood there a moment, staring at the dildo, not too sure about having this thing inside my body because it looked more like a weapon than something used for pleasure. In a swift moment of decision, I stripped down quickly like it was a one night stand waiting for me to act and jumped into bed, sliding between the sheets. I instantly felt uncomfortable, not used to sleeping naked, and couldn't help the tension despite the whiskey I'd drunk.

I needed to name the silly thing, to give it some kind of identity so it didn't feel so foreign. Maybe that would loosen me up. I briefly considered the obvious and, blushing like mad, decided instantly against it. So, not Elliot. Then who?

Gabby crossed my mind, the character whose libido I wished I shared. Maybe thinking about her and her gunslinger would help. I lay there for a while, trying to come up with a scenario, coming up blank for once. I finally heard Jones in my head.

Just get on with it!

Fine, okay then. I was a grown woman and it was a machine. No big deal. And no one ever had to know.

Fumbling under the sheets, not sure what I was doing, I parted my legs, cheeks on fire, and rested it against my bare skin, the silicone feeling a bit sticky. Again I reached for Gabby and fell into her fantasy.

His hands tore at her tunic, ripping it wide, exposing her immense breasts to the chill air. Heavy, strong hands grasped for her, fingers pinching her rigid nipples, his breath catching as she pushed into him, her hands busy under his belt. His face descended, her frustrated fingers losing their place as his hot tongue flicked over one nipple, thumb and forefinger pulling on the other.

She would burst from her need of him, so hot and ready, her mewing gasps begging him to enter her.

My fingers stumbled over the controls and the dildo squealed to life with a very loud

HUMMMMMMMMM. I squeaked in surprise, shocked out of my fantasy, panting and embarrassed all over again. What the hell was that? I pulled it out from under the covers to examine it and found it spiraling in a circle, the hum getting louder. Oh my god, it was so loud, and the walls were thin. Mrs. Barrow was going to hear and ask questions and I wouldn't know what to say.

I spent the next several seconds that felt like forever desperately trying to turn the dildo off, with no luck. Was the stupid controller jammed? The sound seemed to get louder and louder as I panted and fought with it, the motion shifting in mid hum from turning like a music box ballerina to vibrating pulses. I shook it in frustration, hissing at it to shut up. Was I going to have to wait for the batteries to wear out? Or did I have to flush it down the toilet? Hysterical giggles as I mentally pictured explaining to the superintendent why a bright pink dildo was clogging the pipes only made things worse.

My fingers finally found the sweet spot, and not my own. I hit the top button with one last jab of hope and the thing fell silent, dead. I tossed it to the bed, hugging myself and shaking before throwing myself out from under the covers and diving for the closet.

I dressed quickly in my heaviest flannel pajamas, like the thick fabric would hide the fact I'd been toying with something I really wasn't ready for. With a wince and a shudder, I tossed the "thing" into the bottom drawer of my bedside table, determined to throw it out somewhere no one would ever find it or connect it to me.

CHAPTER THIRTEEN

It was hard not to feel defeated, disgusted with myself, as I retreated to the kitchen for some snack therapy, the last of the whiskey burned off by stress. As I stood staring into the bright interior of my fridge, my mind babbled. Maybe being alone wasn't so bad. I could do whatever I wanted, when I wanted. No one could tell me what to do or where to go. How to live my life. Right, sure, that's why I was now contemplating the freezer's contents and the three different tubs of ice cream begging me to devour them. Chocolate won out over vanilla and my weird choice of strawberry that would end up in the trash at some point.

I didn't bother with a bowl, fishing a spoon

out of the clean dishes side of my sink and throwing myself down on the sofa. The TV was the perfect distraction, along with three quarters of a tub of sugary emotional numbness. I prepped to drown myself, dipping my spoon, taste buds exploding on first contact with the sweetness and cold combination.

This had to be better than sex, right? I dove in for another heaping spoon full, searching the listings for something as mindless as chocolate ice cream. Turned out TV wasn't such a great idea. The first show I settled on was a family in turmoil dealing with a child's terminal illness. Great. Next up on Let's Make Mickey Miserable was a movie about a professor having an affair with a student who turns out to be a psycho. Last up for the night, thinking there had to be something happy to watch, I decided on a nature special. Yeah, when the mother bear's first cub died in an accident I turned the TV off, blubbering over what was left of my ice cream.

Tub empty and tissues all over the sofa, I acted on impulse, grabbing my phone and dialing Jones. I wiped the side of my hand across my runny nose while this happy go lucky voice answered my plea. "*Hola, amiga. ¿Cómo estás?*"

Not even her favorite Spanish greeting could make me smile. "Richard is having a baby." I wailed that at Jones, a full on misery wail.

Her reaction was on point and instantly made me feel better. "Oh Mick, I'm so sorry. That asshole."

I spent the next ten minutes pouring out my heart for the second time that night, but this emptying of my hurt at least was met with the familiar and comforting soul who had been there all along, the one person in the world I knew I could trust and go to no matter what. Jones listened, Jones commiserated, Jones swore and called Richard, my mother and Tara names in the perfect places.

Why did that make it feel so much more sorrowful and heart wrenching? When I reached the part about going to the bar, I heard Jones gasp and then laugh.

"Tell me you got drunk and laid in the bathroom and now you're in jail and need me to bail you out." She sounded far too much like she was enjoying this all of a sudden.

"Thanks a lot," I snapped. "Yes, I got drunk, stupidly. God, what is wrong with men? They all just hit on me like I was dinner and they were starving." I shuddered, staring at the empty ice cream carton. "Except Elliot." Damn, how was I ever going to face him again? After everything I said? I felt my poor little heart shrivel and retreat as I realized just what I'd done and that I had to see him at work. Oh god, what had I done?

"Ahem." Jones jerked me back from the brink. "Who, pray tell, is Elliot?" Oh, crap. "I love the name." She sighed like she was thinking naughty thoughts about him which made *me* think naughty thoughts while blushing all over again. "Tell me everything."

"There's nothing to tell," I said, misery returning. "He's hot, he's sweet, and I ruined everything." I told her what I remembered while Jones listened, this time in utter silence. Shocked and appalled at my behavior, likely.

When she finally did speak, after I wound down into a dribble of dejection, she sounded thoughtful, not upset. "I love you, you know that." I nodded like she could see me, snuffling more tears. "But sometimes I want to shake you so hard." So she was pissed at me. "Maybe that would get your head straight for the first time in like, forever." She sighed again, nothing sexual about it, more tired than anything. "You are a catch, my beautiful friend, I just wish you could see that." She was always saying things like that. If I was such a catch, though, Richard wouldn't have cheated, would he? And I wouldn't be pining away after the man who was having a baby with another woman, being mean to men trying to be kind to me, with a fake dick in my bedside table as a sad consolation prize. But Jones wasn't done. "You're smart, and sometimes you're even fun." I snorted a bit of a laugh at that. "You've let your self-esteem be defined by the actions of another person. The *wrong* person. The only one you need to feel worthy of is you. I just wish I could get that through that thick skull of yours."

I didn't respond, unable, unwilling. She was my best friend. Of course she was going to say these things to me, about me. It was just so hard to believe right now.

She must have known I was in a downward spiral. God knew she'd witnessed enough of them in our time as friends. Why did she put up with me again? "Listen here, young lady." Oh boy, that was Jones pulling rank. I knew I was about to get it. "You are going to march that hot hind end over to this guy tomorrow and you are going to ask him out." She'd lost her mind. Lost it completely. "Or at least take him up on his offer to shoot you." How could I after what I'd done, how I'd treated him? "How fucking sexy is *that*?" That was the worst part, didn't she get that? "And you're going to call me as soon as it's done. You hear me? This is for your own good. Get the fucking asshole Richard out of your head. He never deserved you."

I wanted to believe her, to just nod and agree. But I couldn't, not with everything that happened, with my life such a mess, my head whirling with judgment and emotions I couldn't control. "I can't do this right now." I heard her splutter, try to talk over me, but I rushed on, blurted the rest. "I can't... I'm sorry." And, with that, I hung up on my bestie.

Hating myself, hating my life and the disaster I had to face tomorrow and the next day and the next, I dragged myself to bed, burrowed under the covers and willed myself to sleep.

But it wouldn't come and I couldn't stand being me any longer. My only refuge was to retreat into Gabby and her world. I fell into it with open arms, closing off from reality in favor of the woman I wished I was.

His green-gold eyes followed her every movement while her chest heaved with each breath, the pressure intensifying, pushing her breasts against the straining buttons barely holding her shirt together. Any moment now she'd pop right out of the fabric as her aching thighs quivered with anticipation.

"You know I'm yours. If you dare to take me." Her words were barely a whisper but held the heat she struggled to contain inside. In one long stride, as if she'd finally given him what he needed, he stood in front of her, and he wasn't holding back. Long, eager fingers caress her upper arm as the other hand runs rapidly, possessively across her heaving bosom. She inhaled deeply, pressing herself into his touch, her nipples hard from the

contact.

He smiled, head bending toward her, teasing her with his breath, the tip of his tongue tracing between her parted lips. Her swollen nipples ached to be sucked, teased, the thrumming tension between her legs drawing a low growl from her throat.

His index finger complied with her animal-like request, sliding down the front of her shirt, finding her standing at attention. She saw it in his eyes, the moment he lost control, and moaned her excitement as he grasped her shirt in both hands, ripping it open, releasing her straining breasts into his control.

Fabric fell to her waist, moisture surging between her legs. Anticipation an ache she could no longer bear, she grasped him and pulled him tightly against her. His hot, wet mouth suckled first her left, then right breast, inhaling her nipples, transforming them into raging pinpoints of pain and pleasure. A sudden crest of uncontrollable orgasm struck, taking her over the edge, tearing a scream from her throat.

"Take me now!"

CHAPTER FOURTEEN

"**S**eriously, Michaela, what the hell are you doing?"

That was me, berating myself after agreeing to pick up another one of Richard's shirts that he needed desperately this morning. Like yesterday never even happened. "Didn't I say just, last night, no more favors?"

Muttering to myself on the subway didn't get me as many looks as it should have. At least this delivery, another lunch break given up for my ex-husband and his needs, gave me a great opportunity to confront him. Never mind I'd never, ever confronted him about anything before. I was wound up enough I was sure I could do it. Especially with the pregnancy looming huge in my mind. That wasn't going to just go away and neither was I. I needed answers, to understand, at the very least. Though, I was well aware my intention to just ask him straight out would likely peter down to a whining complaint by the time I reached his office because I was that pathetic.

No. I felt my jaw tighten, my hand clenching around the center of his shirt, knowing the pressure would leave wrinkles and so be it. I was marching into his office and demanding answers. He wouldn't know what hit him.

The rest of my ride to his office flew by as I wound what I was going to do over and over in my mind. I didn't remember getting off at the right stop, or the quick walk to his building. Not until I stood at the elevator doors in the lobby did I wake up to where I was. Usually, I started to fret by the time I reached this point, feeling out of place. But this time? An odd and powerful exhilaration raced through me, almost making me giggle out of nervous excitement. Was this me? Yes, yes it was. I deserved to be here. I was owed an explanation and I wasn't going to leave till I was satisfied.

I didn't know this Mickey, but I liked her a lot, the woman who strode past Sheila without even an acknowledgment. I have no idea what expression I wore that created such shock on Richard's assistant's face, but it held her in place behind her desk, silent and staring. I pushed open his door with enough pressure it struck the wall. I almost winced, since I hadn't intended to be that aggressive, but it caught his attention and I was on a roll.

I didn't even bother to close it behind me, not caring if Sheila overheard our conversation or not, if the whole world heard. Three steps carried me to where he sat. I threw his shirt down onto the beautifully crafted desk while he stared up at me with enough guilt he had to know why I was really here.

"When were you going to tell me about the baby?" I couldn't believe I got that question out without sobbing. I felt detached from myself, utterly unemotional about it and pretty damned proud of the fact.

Richard slowly rose, face twisting into concern I doubted instantly. "Michaela." He cleared his throat, circling his desk, reaching for me with one hand. I held my ground, shaking my head, rebuffing his attempt to soothe me. Not this time. Never again. He'd betrayed me for the last time and the monster in front of him? He'd made me.

"I just want to know why, Richard." Was that too much to ask?

His handsome face settled into regret and I felt myself soften slightly. I couldn't let him get to me, not now, not after this unforgivable act. And then he spoke and made it worse. "You know I don't want children." I thought I did. "We talked about this a long time ago." He sagged against his desk, hands gripping the edges as he sat, bringing his face down to my height. "I'm just too busy and it wouldn't be right."

"So you always said." I wasn't giving him an inch, not one tiny scrap of compassion. Even as my heart yielded to his obvious hurt. "Except it's no longer the case, is it?"

"You know I always loved you." Oh god, he had to go there. I clutched at my newfound power and felt it slipping away, the pain taking over as he went on with all that guilt in his voice. "I never meant to hurt you. We just grew apart." Again, so he said. "I swear, I didn't make this choice. Chere wanted it." My heart broke then and there as I absorbed what he meant even before he said it out loud. "I didn't even know she came off her birth control. I was as shocked and angry as you are now." She trapped him into this pregnancy? I wavered, swayed toward him, and he instantly reached out, took my hand while my heart broke for him. Not his fault. Of course not. Who the hell had he married? "This could impact my bid to be partner in the firm." His dream, his goal. How could she? "Even if it doesn't, I won't be home much. A baby will just be a burden." I felt him closing the gap between us more than I was visually aware of it and a moment later his arms were around me. Richard hugged me for the first time in a very long time, that simple, human touch my final melting point.

I was running lava clinging to his volcano, hugging him in return, never wanting to let him go. The last of my strength vanished as the familiar scent of him, the delicious feel engulfed me and, though I hated the tears, I started to cry.

Richard held me a moment before slowly pealing himself free, hands on my upper arms while I blubbered and fought to pull myself together. "I'm so sorry." How horrible for him, how utterly wretched.

He shook his head, letting me go, standing to his full height where he towered over me, like always, face grim. "Please, forgive me. It's done and there's nothing I can do to change it. I never wanted to hurt you, Mick. I swear."

I wanted to tell him I understood, that it wasn't his fault, but I couldn't bring myself to speak again. Instead, I fled, spinning and heading for the door. This time when I passed Sheila I didn't see her expression, didn't care what she thought. My heart was shattered and the agony of it carried me all the way back to work.

As I entered the office, I kept my head down, doing my best not to let anyone see that I'd been crying, even as I caught myself playing back what Richard said while anger returned, burning off the tears. I'd take that blessing. Besides, how dare she? How could Chere force Richard into doing something he so adamantly didn't want? Even while a hint of doubt twinged, the truth that no one could ever make Richard do anything, bit like bile in the back of my throat.

Distracted, confused and struggling with my instincts, I froze as Judy's door slammed open and she emerged, spotting me with a grim look on her face that told me either I was already in trouble or about to be.

"Mickey." She gestured for me to join her. "Get in here."

And my day was just getting better.

CHAPTER FIFTEEN

I needn't have worried, as it turned out, breathing a sigh of relief when my clearly harried boss spun and grabbed a file from the desk, turning to press it into my hands.

"I need you to head down to the Parker's site." Judy was already turning back toward her chair and the messy pile of her own paperwork she was clearly in the middle of. "Elliot needs the specs before he can get started on shooting for the cover." She paused, sipping her coffee, making a face that told me it was likely cold before taking another big gulp, hitting the cushion of her office chair hard enough to make it roll slightly. "Make sure he gets whatever else he needs. I don't have to tell you how good this is for our firm. Front cover of CityLife?" It was only the biggest architectural magazine in the country. I got it. Judy didn't seem to think I did. "This is big Mickey. I need you to follow through on this and keep him happy."

I wondered if she realized that sounded naughty. No, not from her usual no-nonsense attitude she didn't. Still hard for me not to think that was what Judy meant when I had to admit it was what I wanted her to mean.

She didn't even dismiss me, still chugging her coffee and digging into the papers on her desk so I left without a word, closing the door behind me, free hand clutching the file like it was a gift. Even as my heart rattled slightly in my chest as I remembered the embarrassing encounter I'd had with Elliot the night before. Yikes, how was I going to face the gorgeous photographer and not blabber on a huge apology for dumping my life in his lap before running off without much of a thanks for listening?

Then again, I got to see him again, stare into those green-gold eyes. Not a bad assignment, one that meant I also had a field trip ahead of me, always something I looked forward to if only to break up the monotony of my typical day. Yes, I'd had enough excitement of the negative variety. Maybe seeing Elliot again would offer a more positive spin.

The penthouse being renovated by the Parker family had its own private elevator, one I accessed with the key code on the post-it note Judy attached to the front of the file. Because of my job I'd seen many stunning homes, our firm's specialty, the remodel of old buildings turned from neglect to incredible beauty in up-and-coming areas of town always a pleasure. And this particular eight thousand square foot monstrosity was no different. I took a moment as I stepped off the bronze and red tiled elevator to admire the towering twenty foot ceilings of the main foyer in the two story apartment overlooking the river, with a ponderous crystal chandelier casting warm, gold light over the rich brown marble floor. The Parker family had requested the apartment maintain its historic feel, so the glass and metallic look of some of our previous renovations was nowhere in evidence. I personally preferred the antique feel of the place, almost as if I'd stepped into a Hollywood film set.

Movement at the top of the curving staircase caught my attention. I immediately spotted Elliot, leaning over the wood bannister with his camera pointed at me. Instant regret mixed with discomfort almost did me in and I caught myself formulating a blubbering apology. Before I could make an even bigger fool of myself, he raised the camera to his eyes.

"Smile." His voice echoed, as deep and lovely as I remember and I couldn't help myself. His request immediately created the reaction he asked for. At least he wasn't angry with me about last night if his answering smile as he peeked around the side of his camera before returning his attention to the task at hand was any indication. From this distance I could hear the sound of the shutter as he took several photos.

Why did I feel so awkward standing there, still smiling what was surely a goofy grin up at him? I had to break this tension I was feeling or I'd be doing that whole I'm sorry I was an ass routine before too long. "You needed the schematics on the property?" I held up the file as an offering, not just of help but in peace.

"Thank you, I know you're really busy." He sounded genuine enough, still taking pictures. I continued to smile, feeling myself heating up as he followed me with the camera while I climbed the romantic staircase to meet him like I was some starlet on her way to a ball.

Elliot finally lowered his camera, checking the results as he did, when I reached the landing.

I had to say something, anything. "Elliot—"

He shook his head, shrugged, then grinned at me as if he were pleased with my presence instead of being put in charge of a crazy person. Without a word about last night he turned and gestured at the open door leading to a sunlit room on the other side. "Do you mind helping me set dress this area over here? I don't want to take away from the rest of the room because I just love how the natural illumination is creating a glow."

We were going to play never happened, were we? I was all for it, to be honest, chicken enough and equally happy to be in his presence that wiping the slate clean actually appealed to me. I peeked in the door of what had to be some kind of party event room with a large dancefloor and a bar against the far left wall, giant windows leading out to a terrace covered in greenery. I took a moment to appreciate the view while Elliot came to stand next to me, hovering close enough I could smell him, the faint scent of him that had nothing to do with cologne and everything to do with just him. "It's almost surreal, don't you think?" He sounded reverent, happy, and I nodded, agreeing with him, loving that I could see what he saw, that I could share this simple, delighted moment with him. "Want to see through the lens?"

I accepted instantly, my hands rising to take the camera, only to end up holding his big ones, cradling them in mine, the camera a weight that connected us as he settled against me. I was instantly distracted by the warmth of his skin, but excited by this chance to see through his eyes, in a way. He took one step closer, adjusting his body over me so his chest pressed to my shoulder, his hip against mine, heat passing between us. He felt nothing like the creep last night, nothing threatening or dangerous about him, unless dangerous felt like arousal? Discomfort and my natural awkwardness woke up, though I just wanted to turn around and hug him, smell him, see what he felt like as the camera settled against my cheek.

All of my distraction went away when I looked through the viewer, a faint gasp escaping me unbidden. I had to look up at the room before returning to the magical scene he'd framed, using some kind of blurred focus with the central image being the hanging chandelier in the middle of the room.

"It's beautiful." I didn't mean to breathe that out, but I felt honestly breathless.

"It is," he said, intimate, with a faint sigh of his own satisfaction. "One of the most beautiful settings I've photographed in a long time." He waited for me to look up before taking the camera back, though I was actually sad when my hands parted from his. Elliot's faint smile wasn't amused, more sad than anything. "I'm very lucky I get to do what I love for a living."

He was. I thought about writing, my book, and nodded. "You really are."

"Honestly, this job?" He looked around the room again, so much satisfaction and natural charisma on his face I could only stare at him, not the setting, because he was all I could see. "I love it. Devoting myself to photography, to my art? It saved my life."

I didn't know what to say to that, and ended up blurting out, "What do you mean?"

Elliot returned his attention to me, green eyes deep, soft around the edges, quiet and patient. "Before I trusted my talent and went freelance, I was a corporate lackey. Climbing the ladder, chasing my next promotion. You know the type." Did I. I was married to that type for a long time.

"What changed your mind?" I followed him as he guided me toward the bar, not having to hurry to keep up with his long stride. Unlike my ex who would often walk at his fastest pace, forcing me to almost trot to maintain our distance, Elliot took his time, head tilted down and toward me, matching his walk to mine.

"I think I mentioned something about it last night." His eyes twinkled, but there was no judgment and he dropped the subject as he stops at the bar, gesturing for me to go behind it. "I want to see some action shots, if you don't mind playing bartender?"

CHAPTER SIXTEEN

I did as I was asked without question, actually eager to do so. Turned out I was a great assistant, at least according to Elliot. His soft banter and easy way of being, while professional, was equally friendly and put me at ease. Before too long we were laughing and chatting and my tension was gone, as if last night never happened. All the while he explained lighting, what made a shot interesting for him, finding that one perfect moment that it all came together to make the whole experience fulfilling. I found myself enthralled in every word and absolutely fascinated by his job, his manner and his natural confidence.

So easy to equate his utter joy in his job with mine for writing while making me wonder why I hadn't yet finished my book. I couldn't remember smiling so much ever. Elliot was a fantastic teacher, whether he was aware of it or not, bringing out my creative side. When I suggested trying some angled shots of one of the bedrooms, his enthusiasm for the idea made me blush.

"You're a natural, Mick," he said, standing on a chair in his sock feet to get the look he wanted. I wondered if he realized I was aware he framed me in the shot? "You should come work for me."

I knew he was joking, but still, it made me feel appreciated and I beamed at him in response. I languished in his encouragement, following him around for the next hour or so, offering ideas when he asked but loving observing him at work, like watching a painter or a sculptor tease perfection out of nothing.

When I slipped and almost dropped a vase he'd asked me to move, he caught me with the kind of quick skill that told me he'd been paying attention to where I was, what I was doing, and for the moment I felt his arm around me, supporting me and then guiding me back upright while I blushed and stammered an apology, I realized for the first time I felt utterly safe with him. As if I could trust him completely, no matter what, unguarded and exposed. Since I'd already dumped my life on him, it might not have been an unusual response to his kindness and focus, but still. It was a strange feeling. Had I not felt safe for a while?

I realized then I hadn't, especially not with a man. I had to admit, in that sun-drenched penthouse with that gorgeous man who didn't judge, didn't belittle and offered sweet smiles and gentle praise that I'd been on edge when it came to men since I'd met Richard.

I caught myself growing bolder, asking questions of his choices of shots. My every question was answered with enthusiasm and joy. That, in turn, fueled me to ask more, until I glanced at my watch and realized it had been hours since I arrived, almost 5PM, as we danced around the penthouse's giant footprint light's shooting, talking. It was magical and I hated to see it end.

I wanted to remember this feeling. Like a precious creation I needed to protect. Elliot himself seemed only then to notice the time, packing up his gear with some regret.

"Thank you," I said. "I had an amazing afternoon." Was that a weird thing to say? I instantly judged it but Elliot's laugh told me he didn't.

"I'd work with you in a heartbeat, given the chance." He straightened from his camera bag, slinging it over his shoulder, standing over me again. This time I didn't feel intimidated or uncomfortable in his presence, despite his stunning looks. Instead, a warmth had come to live inside me, a familiarity that gave me confidence around him, enough I beamed back and believed he truly meant what he said. "You have a great eye for detail, a different way of looking at things than I do. I like it, Mick."

My heart did a soft hiccup, a wriggling flip of delight. This was the most praise I'd received in one sitting since I was, what, six? I had an odd thought that stilled my surge of joy as I realized the last person to make me feel this happy was my father. But wait, that same man my mother maligned every time I saw her? No way. He'd abandoned me, abandoned us when I was just a little girl. So weird to think of Dad like he was my hero, not the asshole who left me behind.

I shook off that odd little trip down memory lane and chose to focus on the man in front of me. "Thank you, Elliot." I stuttered as I realized I didn't just mean for today. "For everything. Thank you." His slow, quiet nod seemed expectant, like he was waiting for more. But what? "I'm going to head back to the office and check in. See you later?"

He didn't answer for a moment. Was that disappointment in his eyes? But he was still smiling, a perpetual expression for him, apparently, and when he spoke his voice was warm, inviting. "Most definitely Mickey. I would like that very much." He paused before touching my cheek with his fingertips, tucking some hair back behind my ear in a strangely sweet gesture that would have triggered my anxiety from another man. "And thank *you*. I really enjoyed my shoot today, more than ever, because you were here."

It was hard to leave, but I did it, riding the elevator alone when he took a call and waved goodbye as he answered. I was literally skipping when I left the building, had to pull myself under some semblance of control, though a girlish giggle escaped me several times, ending in breathless sighs as I ran over the last few hours in Elliot's presence.

Nothing could bring me down after that amazing experience. Not Mom, not Tara. Richard? Hell no. In fact, Elliot had set a fire in me, the drive to write, to finish my book, to claim the kind of excited happiness he had for photography I knew I could feel for being a novelist.

The chains held her captive but his touch was going to set her free. If only he could reach her! She strained against the icy rock at her back, calling his name, while he swung his

heavy sword, dark hair hanging over his blue eyes blazing with fire, cutting through the banshees hovering around her prison.

The hideous creatures with women's faces and the bodies of filthy vultures screamed their rage at his attack, their sagging breasts oozing toxic bile, their pointed teeth flashing in the moonlight. She shivered, her dress wet from falling snow, the shackles biting into her flesh, the damp cloth clinging to her body, exposing her taunt figure as her bosom heaved in response to his heroic rescue.

I couldn't stop smiling as I entered the office, heart and mind lost in the fantasy I might dive into rather than the book I had been working on for too long. Did I dare abandon Gabby, though? Then again, maybe she was holding me back and a bit of exploration of new voices might be just the thing I needed. For the first time I could see possibilities, no longer trapped by that single idea I'd been writing and rewriting and deleting for so long. It helped I was feeling sexier than I've ever felt, more connected to that side of me and the romance I was meant to be writing.

I slid into my chair and logged onto my computer to check my emails, not realizing until I did Paul was still at his desk. Weird, he was usually gone right at five and it was already quarter past.

His wheels squeaked as he pushed his chair next to mine. I looked up, dread at having to deal with him right now dulling a bit of my enthusiasm. Made worse when I met his eyes and saw he wasn't his usual grinning, gossiping self. He actually looked upset.

"Just an FYI," he said, anger in his voice, "I've been made point on the Randall account. You know, the one you handed in to Lauren yesterday, claiming you corrected my work." I gaped at him, my stomach clenching in angry response. "You might have to actually be at work to help finish the project, you know, rather than running off on whatever personal errands you think are more important all afternoon." He leaned closer, as he spoke again. "What with job security on the line?" Wait, what? "Make sure you check in with me next time or I'll have to report you to Judy."

CHAPTER SEVENTEEN

"Excuse me?" I sputtered that question, stunned, not quite sure what I was hearing. My body wanted to get up and walk into Judy's office despite the fact she'd be long gone by now while my brain held me in one place, second guessing.

"Oh Mick, you know I'm the right man for the job." His leering wink wasn't as forgivable as usual while resentment woke and burned a little hole in my middle. "Don't you worry, I've got the account handled, as long as you pull your weight." As long as I...? I couldn't breathe, wanted to protest, to shoot back I was the one who fixed his mistakes, but he was still talking and I couldn't seem to put two words together. "I've already called over to that photographer. It's better if I handle him from now on, you know his type." The urge to sink further into my chair rode over me as I wondered if Paul somehow read my mind or knew just how much my afternoon with Elliot had given me. "Guys like him think they can swoop in and take advantage of our staff like this is a singles club or something." Was that jealousy in his eyes? Yes, yes it was. "Just makes me so angry." His chair rolled a little bit closer, blocking me against my cubical wall, the intimacy of his presence suddenly all kinds of awkward. "Anyway, you know I have your back, right? Always have."

I couldn't believe I was about to agree, the automatic nod starting even as his hand landed on my knee and squeezed. My stomach rolled over and I choked on a protest.

"Elliot's not like that." I could see it was the wrong tact to take, the wrong direction to turn the conversation toward, but all I could think about was spending that magical afternoon in sunlight and joy with the handsome photographer who treated me like no man had ever treated me before. I managed to keep myself from gushing, at least I think I did. I instantly gauged my own tone as more words of defense tumbled out. "He's actually very cool, Paul." Yes, that sounded reasonably casual.

From the look on Paul's face, I was about as transparent as his hand on my leg. "See! You're distracted already." He shook his head, squeezing a little harder, hand climbing just a fraction. "No wonder I needed to take over the project. You have to keep your head in the game." I was seriously going to throw up. "Don't let Mr. Suave get you into trouble at work. You need this job right? I mean, you didn't get anything from the other loser. I'm only looking out for you." His words made sense but as he talked his fingers rubbed against my skin. All kinds of alarms sounded off in my brain while I fought against the fact he was right. Besides, this was Paul. He was harmless, wasn't he?

I forced myself to relax, despite hating the act I had to play. "Congratulations on the account," I said. "Whatever you need." Did I really just kowtow? Yes, yes I did. Even while I turned my chair just enough away from his it forced him to drop his hand from my leg. Paul didn't fight that move, still smiling and I found myself exhaling softly past my discomfort. Seriously, I was way overreacting. He'd never done anything that would feel seriously threatening. And the whole project takeover thing, blaming me for not doing work he'd messed up? Yeah, that story wasn't new. I'd been the fall guy for almost everyone in the office over the years. That was my fault, not his.

Paul stood at last, grabbing his suit jacket, pulling it on while he stared at me. "I sent you an email with what I need done for tomorrow. Considering you were gone all afternoon, I'm sure you won't mind staying to get it done. Night, Mick."

He left without another word, striding out of the office like he ruled the world while I stared after him, wishing I had the guts to just leave and not care about this job. That part at least he was right about. Even if I didn't enjoy what I did, I needed this position, single woman and all.

Letting myself fume at my own lack of confidence on the inside, I turned to check the email he'd sent, determined to prove to myself, at least, I was a team player. Never mind it was Judy herself who'd sent me out today. I'd probably outstayed my assignment helping Elliot the way I had, so even trying for that excuse would likely end up with me in Judy's office apologizing to Paul. No way, not happening. Instead, I buckled down and tackled the job at hand.

I did like this part of my job, actually. Paul had assigned me to organizing the rest of the project by timelines, very much like creating chapters in a book before I started to write. I found it engrossing, the planning and projected end result that gave me a satisfied feeling when I finally hit send on the completed job.

It was almost 7PM when I looked up from my computer. I felt invisible tucked into my small workspace, usually comfortable but suddenly lonely. At least I was finally done for the day, though I hated the feeling I had inside that I was slinking out after everyone else like the bad girl who'd been put into detention because she'd done something wrong.

Home was as quiet and isolating as the office and for the first time I felt out of sorts in my little apartment, like I needed to get outside again. Instead, I set my teapot out and, leaning against the counter with one hip, wearily wondered how my day had gone to crap like it did.

I should have told Paul that he was wrong and I was going to work with Elliot. I had already done a great job saving his butt with Lauren, only to have him take over that account like it had been my fault not his. Besides, Judy sent me to work with the photographer. Maybe if I talked to her she'd let me carry on with him. He certainly seemed to enjoy having me around. I played out some scenarios in my head, all of them working out with me winning and Elliot falling utterly in love with me while Paul begged my forgiveness, Lauren wanted to be my friend and Judy retired, giving me her job and office all while the teapot whistled at me for my attention.

I finally poured myself a nice peppermint blend and carried it to the sofa. Feet up, I inhaled the aromatic drink like it was a magic elixir, that first taste ready to make all my wishes come true. I caught myself smiling at that thought and I closed my eyes, wishing reality went the way my fantasies did. I could be anything, do anything, have anyone I wanted. Instead, as I opened my eyes again and studied the old water stain on the ceiling, I felt that crushing sense of failure I'd fought since I was a teenager, that same feeling that rode me to accept that there were things in life I just couldn't change, remind me I wasn't the woman who got to live the life my dreams were made of.

Instead of falling into the dark well of unhappiness, though, this time I found my eyes losing focus, that pair of gorgeous green ones appearing in my memory. My lips curved into a smile, hands clutching the hot mug while in my mind I tried out an all-new scenario.

I stood from my desk and approached Lauren's, Elliot's laugh coming to an abrupt halt as he saw me. I let him catch the heat in my gaze, but walked past instead of stopping, making sure to lightly brush up against him as I did, hips swaying while I dropped a coy sideways smile.

I heard him excuse himself, the sound of footfalls pursuing me, that feeling of cat and mouse sending goosebumps of desire over my entire body. I paused at the elevator, knowing he was close behind me as he came to a stop in my tracks, so near the heat of him registered against my back. My body reacted, tense and ready for his touch. As the door opened he joined me, his hand settling just barely on my waist. Sparks flared between us and my body quivered in response. His hand traveled down my hip, absorbing my heat while sharing his own. I was on fire and as I turned to look up at him, the doors closing behind us, I saw in his face I wasn't the only one. I was an open flower waiting for his honey bee to drink my nectar.

I faced him with my back against to wall. He hit the emergency button all the while drowning me in his gaze, his stare never leaving mine. My breathing tooks on a life of its own, intense and demanding. My huge breasts ached, begging to escape their confines, to leap loose from their prison, to feel his hands, his mouth, his breath.

Instead of giving me what I needed, he just stood there, drinking me in, until a low growl escaped his lips. "What do you want?"

Delicious, that question, like ripe fruit as tasty as the acts I wanted him to perform. My throat felt dry and craved for him to quench me. I reached out and grabbed the front of his shirt, slow but demanding, and pulled him toward me. When his lips were over mine, hovering, his body so close I was desperate for him, I speak.

"You."

His mouth met mine with the kind of terrifying fever that devoured while it flared. His hands ran down my arms without touching, building even more electricity between us. I could feel my body open, my legs spreading, hands grasping for his hips. I jerked him toward me, pushing my groin into his already protruding bulge.

"I need to see what's under there," I whispered as I touched and stroke his member.

Elliot groaned and seemed to lose all control. I panted every breath while he ripped my shirt wide open, buttons flying free as he exposed my perfect, soft flesh, my nipples so ready for him to eat, like huge, ripe cherries.

"I want you to eat them." My hands grasped his hair, pulling his head down toward me while he moaned and dove in, mouth eager, hot, wet. "Suck them raw. Peel them with your tongue." He expertly complied with my demands, the sensation of his lips, teeth, tongue driving me wild, sending waves of shuddering intensity through me. One of his big hands found my waist band, the button and zipper on my skirt, and navigated down inside the now loose fabric while I pushed against his hot mouth and thrust my hips toward his seeking fingers. So much heat, I could barely stand it, a volcano ready to erupt between my legs. I groan from want. "Touch me, please touch me."

Elliot's mouth rose, captured mine, sucking and biting my lips as he pinned me to the wall, entire body pressing me tight to the hard surface. The work he'd done on my nipples had built enough lust to overtake every sense. I was melting together, a blazing inferno of need and passion, my own hands trapped between us, firm strokes of his own pulsing need only feeding mine.

My hips moved toward his fingers, trying to force contact on my terms. When he gave in and the tip of his index finger finally made contact with my clitoris I screamed, shudder, entire being awake to him. His fingertip rotated small, circular motions around the erect nub, wave after wave of vibrating sensation taking me to the edge and back again, never letting me peak, so close I softly begged in panting breaths for release.

And then we were tearing at the rest of our clothes, both of us in equally savage passion. I needed him desperately, inside me, our bodies meant to be one. And when he thrust into my *waiting well, we fit perfectly, gliding together as if made for one another. His gorgeous cock filled me, sending giant ripples of pure pleasure through me, surges of sensation overtaking me while I pulled him tightly to me and rocked against his heaving hips.*

My legs wrapped around his lean strength, hands cupping his perfect ass as we pushed off the wall in unison. I'd never been fucked like this before, so deep, his tip massaging my cervix, rocking up and down, my fingers finding my own clit and increasing the pleasure. My nipples rubbed against the light hair on his broad chest, the sensation only adding more tension in my body. Delicious. And—

And. I sat up, blinking, feeling the pulsing between my legs, heat rising in my cheeks while the orgasm took me over and rode the soft wave to conclusion. I laughed a little, staring down into my cold tea and feeling embarrassed by the entire fantasy, wondering how I'd ever look Elliot in the face now. Maybe Paul dealing with him was a good thing. And yet, I couldn't wait to see the handsome photographer again.

Elliot walked toward me. "Do you have a minute?

CHAPTER EIGHTEEN

I opened my eyes and threw myself out from under the covers for the first time in, well, ever. The fantasy had played itself out with me finally going to bed and falling into a deep, happy sleep that did nothing to kill the tingling of excitement in my body and spirit. My morning pot of coffee felt unnecessary for the first time. And, as I inhaled the aroma of the familiar brew, I found I was actually ready to log in and kick some butt on the book percolating equally in my mind.

Yes, Thursday was crap. Friday, a mixed bag. Saturday? I got this.

I settled into my chair with my laptop on the small desk I'd splurged on, my writing nook carefully prepared for weekends diving deep into creativity. My typical ritual had me logging in with my writing circle. I'd joined a few months ago, using the supportive gaggle of fellow writers to help me stay on point. It was genius, really, and I checked in that the other dozen or so active members had already registered their Saturday goals.

I happily created my own post. *I'm starting my character Gabby, her scenario, but this time it's going to be set on the open seas with the captain saving the duchess Gabby from these pirates about to attack her ship.* I second guessed, another idea taking hold. *There is a stable boy watching Gabby and her escort playing in the hay around the horses.* Hmmm. That wasn't doing it for me, either. I'd tried that one before. *Gabby is held prisoner, chained to the dungeon wall while this man in black is about to have his way with her.* I hit delete yet again and pondered before typing. *Gabby is in her bedchambers anticipating her lover, she's terribly excited to see what new and naughty things he's going to do to her tonight.*

I deleted one last time before sitting back, frowning at the laptop screen, fifteen minutes gone into my precious writing time and nothing striking the right chord. I couldn't decide, the truth of that frustrating. Nothing seemed right. Had I somehow burned up my creative energy last night, thinking about Elliot?

No, I had to admit my clandestine time with the imaginary photographer wasn't the problem. It was the same old fear, the fact no one would be interested in any of what I had to offer. How many Saturdays had I wasted writing and deleting, writing and deleting while pretending to work on my book?

I was such a fraud. What did I know about being a romance writer? I scowled at my coffee, chest tight, throat aching. How could I write about love and sex when I had no idea what it was outside my fantasies? Did I even know what great sex was? I shook my head at myself, thinking about Richard. He'd been my one and only. And honestly, the imaginary lovemaking I'd had with Elliot last night? Way better than any groping and grunting time I'd spent under my ex-husband before he'd finished and rolled over and left me to wonder if that was all there was.

I ended up staring at my white screen, frustrated and hating this moment. I used to love writing. Why was it so hard all of a sudden?

The timer dinged, my writing group chiming in on their stats while I realized I'd wasted the entire hour sitting there, feeling sorry for myself. I cringed, intimidated on so many levels. JJ was at two chapters. MizzyMae was scoring 3500 words. HandyMomma worked out a plot hole and was editing. I checked in with a lie, hating myself as I typed.

1k in and still at it!

Their supportive replies only made me feel worse. Knowing it was foolish, that I was really only lying to myself, I logged off instead of trying to go another hour. What was I actually accomplishing, anyway? Instead of abandoning writing all together, I opened my blog, *Divorced Life* and review my last post. Originally I started it to document my new and improved life. Not bitter to discover there was nothing new and improved about it or anything. With only two posts in six months there really wasn't much chronicling going on. Nothing ever happened to me that felt worthy of recording.

"New and improved, my ass." I fired off that complaint to Zeus. His little cactusness ignored me, as always. Adding salt to the wound, I had exactly zero followers. Zip, nadda, no one.

The urge for junk food hit like a barrage of inspiration. Like eating crap would snap my creativity into high gear. It wasn't hard to talk myself into a day of movies, sweet and salty snacks and, as I blushed over the memory and sudden eagerness to revisit last night's activities, Elliot time. Because, if I was going to be totally honest with myself, food wasn't the kind of sweet and salty I was craving.

My corner store was only a block away so I didn't bother changing from my comfy red heart flannel pajamas. I barely remembered to brush my teeth and my hair was a total bypass, but it wasn't like the little old lady who ran the cash register cared what I looked like.

It didn't take me long to make my comfortable way to the shop just before noon, to find my favorite treats or carry them in half-stupor to the counter. I shuffled from one foot to the other, absently scratching at my stomach through the gap between the buttons of my pajama top, mind winding around last night's interesting ideas while I caught myself blushing about just how happy my body had been with the entire process.

I'd never had that kind of resolution with Gabby's stories. In fact, I'd always reached a point where I'd gotten kind of bored with her unfolding tales and tried a new one on for size. Maybe that was the problem? Maybe I needed to start writing from a different point of view? Something more immediate and personal? I bit my lower lip as I grinned at the idea of writing something from my own perspective. Not that I'd keep it that way. I could easily shift it to a character's voice after I was done, right? I found myself nodding at the idea, contemplating writing when I got home and excited by the prospect, even as a voice interrupted.

"Big plans for this afternoon?"

Oh. My. God. Shock and dread and the overwhelming need to sink into a hole in the ground didn't stop me from turning around. Only to have my wide eyes lock on those familiar green-gold ones even as my entire body froze.

CHAPTER NINETEEN

I had to escape but there was no ducking out, not while I stood two feet from the gorgeous creature I'd spent all night last night fantasizing about. I didn't mean to, but I'm sure I probably looked like Elliot was a leper and I didn't want to contract his disease.

Anyone else would have treated me like the crazy person I'd obviously turned (back) into, gaping at him and blushing that slow, steady heat of embarrassment that took my breath away. Instead, in just the right amount a gentle Elliot, he grinned and winked.

"How is your Saturday?"

I wanted to hide, die, run away, be swallowed by the ground beneath my feet.

Something, anything, dear lord save me now. Instead, I inhaled and blurted out a string of I don't remember what, my usual vomiting of too much information I'd never remember I said while my brain moaned, "Why did he have to be here, him of all people? Why can't I just be normal around him?"

Meanwhile, my mouth ran away with me. "I had a great start to my day. I was all gung-ho, you know," as I used my fist as an exclamation mark because I was a total weirdo. "Always starting off with all these good intentions. I even checked in with my writing group. They are all such prolific writers." Stop talking, Mickey. Just stop talking. "I wish I could be more like them." And a-rambling I went. "I started a couple different chapters, but I wasn't really creating the flow I was hoping for, you know?" Did he nod like he actually was interested? Because even I wasn't interested as I desperately threw down my purchases on the counter and silently begged the cashier to just hurry up already. "I'm on track for a new idea, though, so I'm going to set a new deadline." Intro Big Picture Screen Smile meant to look truthful while making my cheeks ache from the lie. And then, the final blurt, the piece de resistance, the nail in my self-built coffin because I just couldn't stop talking. "I started a blog!"

Disclosure regret was immediate and

crushing. Why did I tell him that? I wasn't expecting the strong reaction from him, how he moved closer to me with a massive grin.

"Really? That's fantastic. What did you call it? I'd love to follow." He pulled out his phone, opened his browser, waited, expectant while I died inside.

Hello, backpedaling. "It's a work in progress." No judgement in his eyes, at least, just patience while I inhaled, exhaled and spoke my first truth. "I wanted to document my new life after, you know, Richard and let other women know it's ok to go through the 'D' word." He waited patiently, letting me talk. Funny, Richard never let me talk. I found myself actually warming to the topic, feeling the real me bubble to the surface while my awkwardness faded away. "It's called *Divorced Life*, but I can change that. As I move through my life. You know?"

His smile told me he did, imagine that. "I used to be an architect with a huge firm in Chicago. I mentioned it yesterday, I think." I nodded in response like one of those bobble dolls with a hula dress, except mine was red heart flannels. "It was just about the number at the end of the day." He leaned against the counter while the cashier handed me change and my plastic bag of goodies. I barely remembered her asking for money, let alone finishing the transaction while Elliot went on.

"It was awful, Mick. Like my spirit was totally broken."

I nodded again, change damp in my palm while I squeezed it tight and fought the urge to tell him I knew exactly how he felt. Since when did I feel that way? I had to admit, it was an ongoing thing. "That's when my marriage started to fall apart." I gaped at him as he laughed slightly, not bitter but not happy, either. I actually felt closer to him than ever, knowing he was divorced, too. Someone as gorgeous and awesome as him? Made me feel a bit better about myself.

He was far from done, though. "When it did, boy, it crashed and burned fast." Elliot handed the cashier the pack of razors in his hand. His big, capable hand that fished cash out of his wallet. I couldn't stop staring at those long, strong fingers until he spoke again. "But I didn't care. Does that make sense?" God, did it. More mute nodding as we moved away from the counter to let other shoppers have their turn, that same hand I was admiring now resting lightly on my elbow. "I was miserable already, craving something creative." Like me and writing. Except he'd made something of his need.

Elliot's smile returned, the real, happy one. "I used to love building, when it was about the beauty of the piece. There's nothing else like it in the world, seeing your creation standing in full magnificence." I had that same longing, to see my name on the cover of a real live published novel. "But then it turned into how fast could I move up? Hopefully without someone behind me ready to trip me on the way by." Paul's face flashed in my head, Lauren's. Were Elliot and I really so parallel? "I needed something else."

I swallowed, wanted to ask questions, but Elliot was still talking like I'd cracked open some treasure chest of knowledge with the simple act of being real with him and I wasn't about to interrupt, not when he guided me outside and headed down the street, no longer touching me but heading in the right direction. Not that I would have corrected him. I would have walked for hours with him if he'd just keep talking.

"I was asked to go to an art show about two years ago." That pensive look was about as endearing as it got. "I don't remember the specifics, but I do remember seeing this certain artist's work of city scenic shots. I was hooked." Brilliant, that smile, stunningly radiant like the sun coming up. I wished I could feel that happy, just once, jealous suddenly for his surge of joy. "I literally fell in love with all of it. My family and coworkers thought I was crazy. I quit my job and jumped into photography." A casual shrug, a knowing lip-twist like he assumed I'd heard the same about my writing from those around me. Except he was living the dream and I was just faking it. "I'm great at covering buildings because of my background. It's like I can see their hearts, somehow, hear the beat of their soul." Jealousy be gone, I wanted to hug him and absorb him in the hope he'd rub off on me. Handsome and sexy, yes, but full of something else I craved. Happiness. "Thankfully others see what I see through my work. I'm able to translate it. So they hire me. I have never been so happy."

The sight of my front stoop stopped me in my tracks while Elliot laughed and turned to keep going, walking backwards. "My hotel is just around the corner, like I said the other night." I duck my head, remembering being drunk and stupid and confrontational but he still wasn't judging me, imagine that, so I smiled and looked up at him while he paused. "I'm here for a few more days, then I'm off."

"Where?" How could a single sentence from a man I barely knew feel so incredibly crushing?

"Europe, probably." He swung the plastic bag in his hand with a sort of child-like innocence. "I've had a ton of work there. I guess I'm kind of known now, and it's easy on my creativity. So much to shoot."

He was about to go. I could feel it, knew Elliot planned to say goodbye, to walk away and that would be it. My only real chance to encourage him to continue the conversation would be lost to Paul and my awkwardness. The air was suddenly thick, the kind that made my tongue feel heavy. Mick. Say *anything*.

Except it wasn't me who spoke up. "Would you like to have dinner before I go?"

Was it possible to explode from sheer excitement and gratitude? Maybe not, but I was about as close as anyone ever got to it, I think. I seriously thought my face was going to burst open from the giant smile that split my mouth in half. "Yes," couldn't leap past my lips fast enough.

"Do you want me to call you?" Those eyes, though.

"Yes." I giggled. Actually giggled, like a little kid.

Elliot's answering laugh was infectious and though I knew there was no real reason to feed the good humor when he closed the distance between us again, phone in hand, we were both chuckling.

I gave him my number, wishing I had my own phone with me, plenty of room in the pockets of my giant pajama bottoms. Yikes, what was I wearing? While Elliot finished entering my number I made myself a promise. The next time he laid eyes on me? He wouldn't know what hit him.

Elliot sent me a text with his first name so

I'll recognize his number and tucked his phone away while my mind not only swooned over the fact he's a gentleman but logged that activity for the new book I was writing. The book about him. And me.

"I'll see you soon, then." Surely I could have come up with a better goodbye? I smiled and watched him as I walked backwards toward my front steps. The adorable and funny thing? He was doing the same. With a final wave, I turned, feeling like I was floating, barely remembering the climb to the front door, the ride on the elevator.

The sensation of weightlessness stayed with me the rest of the way to my front door. Just as I reached for the nob, Mrs. Barrow violently swung open her own, thrusting something at me.

"Missed one." She coughed, roughly handing the object to me, scratching my skin with her dry, bony hands, then slammed her door.

I stared down at the package, wondering what it could be. Same label, from the toy company. But I'd only ordered one? Wait, there was a C/O on the label.

Jones. What did she buy for me that night? Heart beating a bit faster in curious anticipation, worried it might end as badly as the first encounter with the horrible thing in my nightstand, I carried the box inside.

CHAPTER TWENTY

L aughing to myself, I threw the box on the sofa, heading to the kitchen for a pair of scissors. I was surprised to find I wasn't as nervous as when I opened the original box, instead rather eagerly investigating the contents. And, to my surprise, I had to admit I was highly aware of how oversensitive my body felt.

The tiny device seemed unintimidating compared to the giant dildo, a small egg shape in chrome with a cute remote control complete with a simple on/off switch and a dial to control the speed. Blushing but determined, I headed toward my bedroom.

I took a few moments to get the hang of it

after installing batteries in the remote, the egg itself already charged according to the literature in the box. Last time I'd been in a hurry, feeling awkward and uncomfortable, but today? Today I had Elliot on my mind, a full evening of fantasy with him under my belt and a pending date I refused to ruin by being a prude. I chose to strip off slowly this time, catching my reflection in the mirror. Like I was putting on some kind of sexy show, my flannels in one hand as I twirled them in the air before I let them fly. It was cooler now and my body reacted to the day's crispness, not yet time to turn on the heat but far enough into late October I needed a quilt to sleep. The temperature shift from the warmth of my pajamas to the cooler air invoked a sensuous reaction from me and, giggling at my own bravery, I took a moment to run my hands over my naked skin, admiring myself in the mirror.

Sure, I wasn't a supermodel or anything. I knew I was carrying about twenty pounds too many for the front cover of a magazine and maybe I could have been hitting the gym instead of the snacks, but all in all? Yeah, I was hot.

I didn't even get into bed this time, instead stretching out on the quilt, exposed to the room, refusing to let nerves stop me from having this private fun. Who would judge me?

Only me, and I was done with that. I fell into the memory of his eyes, those eyes that looked straight into my soul. As my mind wound around him, I turned on my new friend.

It took me a moment to find the right spot, but when I did? The instant vibration hit my clitoris, I was lost. It felt as if I'd been waiting for this, for the sensations that rippled across my lower abdomen, that tightened between my thighs, the aching waves of pleasure hitting me like a tsunami. I gasped in surprise then laughed out loud and settled into the growing sensations. The toy helped me stay on point while I thought of Elliot's handsome face, his strong arms and what he could do to me. About what his cock could do.

That gorgeous beast would rip me apart.

The top of the pleasure wave started to take me, far too fast, out of my control. It felt completely different from last night's experience, hot and sharp and with a gasping tingling that peaked in a rush, devouring my hips and thighs and that tight, hot, aching between my legs in a surge of heat and electricity. My whole body convulsed, heart racing, all rational thought gone as my head lifted off my pillow, back arching in response to the flare of fire. My free hand collected a handful of quilt and I held my breath as the final rise of orgasm took me, shook me, and finally let me go.

Suddenly I couldn't bear to have the vibration touch my clitoris, the sensation far too intense and I groaned a little, shutting it off while I lay back and panted out a few breaths. I could feel the heat of my face as if I'd run a marathon, heart unclenching even as softly pulsing contractions eased at the mouth of my vagina.

I released my hand from the quilt, fingers aching, but I wasn't complaining. I laughed out loud, for once not caring if anyone heard me. Without thinking I jumped out of bed, throwing on my pajamas again before heading for the kitchen and the kettle. I propped open my laptop and, in a frenzy of excitement and lingering passion, I dove deep into Gabby's world.

She'd been in fear of not only her purse but her body as well as the trio of bandits leaped from the forest and pulled her from her horse. At least her faithful steed lingered, the mare snorting and pawing the ground just a few feet away, keeping out of the reach of the desperate, filthy man trying to capture her as he and his cohorts had captured her mistress. Gabby gasped a breath, putting her back to a tree but knowing she stood no chance against three assailants.

She was sure she'd have been a victim of their lecherous intent if not for the handsome gentleman with such presence and confidence that when he rode at a gallop into their midst the bandits could only stare when his stallion came to a rearing halt. His rapier sang when he drew it from horseback, saying, "Be off, you thieves. This lady has a champion."

Gabby's tightly bound bosom heaved so greatly she feared she would expose herself, shocked to find the thrill of the attack so extremely erotic. She knew it wasn't sane to feel such things, but she couldn't deny how her body reacted. One look at the gentleman and his superior arms—a sword and horse versus their small, rusted knives and on foot no less— and the ruffians turned and fled.

Gabby, for her part, had already forgotten their attack, focused on her rescuer. She gazed up at his great height, deep into the most amazing green eyes, gloved hands pressed to her still heaving chest. "Thank you, sir. I know not how to ever repay you."

To her delight, he'd bowed deeply in the saddle before dismounting, towering over her, dark hair in waves to the collar of his crisp, white shirt, cascading over the velvet of his deep green coat. "To know you are unharmed, dear lady, and that I was in time to assist is all the thanks I need." He glared down the path, rapier sheathed yet again. "The King shall hear of this. It's unfortunate such men are permitted to threaten the innocent of our land."

He collected her horse, helped her mount, one large hand at the small of her back. She felt the thrill of his touch, wanting it again as much as she feared that of the bandits, wondering at her sudden wanton state. But it made her bold, the memory of her fallen husband's caress a faint whisper of what it felt like to be a real woman, and she spoke up before she could stop herself.

"Sir, you have rescued Gabriella De Minto, Lady of Greymoore." His eyebrows arched at her admission. So he'd heard of her? Many had, since it was her dead husband who'd saved the life of the king some three years ago, giving his own to ensure their monarch survived an assassin's attack. "May I invite you to dinner? I couldn't in good conscious not at least feed my gallant hero."

"I would be honored, madam." He made sure she was secure in her saddle before mounting himself. "My name is Michael, Lord of Colliet. May I escort you home?"

Their horses met, came together, the mare close enough to heat, Gabby knew, the stallion's attempt to nip her neck would lead to more if they were allowed to remain in contact. Again the reminder of what she'd lost, the passing of her noble husband still poignant. But it had been a long three years without his attentions and in that time she'd never felt the pull toward anyone, to fill that need with another.

Until now.

She almost laughed at the stallion's antics, at her savior's flushing, his stammered apologies when the giant black beast he rode exposed the massive penis, ready for her mare. Nor did she say out loud she longed for his teeth on her flesh or even that large offering pulsing between his horse's legs, the counterpart she knew the handsome man beside her bore beneath his breeches. Oh, she was wicked, and lonely. Perhaps that could be remedied.

The manor house welcomed them, the quiet of the stable yard only broken by the boy who collected their steeds. "Please come in, my lord." She didn't wait to see if he followed, hearing his footfalls on the cobbles, then the steps, joining her inside.

"Michael," he said, voice low. "You can call me Michael."

"Then please, allow me the same courtesy. I am Gabriella."

As they sat down for the hastily prepared dinner her staff assembled, Gabby couldn't help but notice the lovely bulge under his coat hem, comparing that to the much smaller one she'd been privy to with her husband. How would that feel between her legs? She couldn't help blushing, though she caught herself leaning over, exposing the depth of her cleavage, wishing he would touch her, all the while asking the most mundane questions.

"Where are you from? What brought you to this part of the country, and at such an ideal moment?"

She was sure he was aware of what she offered, she was being blatant enough about it, surely. The intensity of his gaze, the way his eyes dipped to skim over her breasts, the way his broad shouldered body settled deeper into his seat, had to be indications of his arousal. Matched to hers?

He sipped his drink, full lips wet from the liquor. "I ride to join the king as his new advisor," he said. "I have been blessed with the position, thanks to my father's history with our monarch and my own experience on the battlefield."

A war hero, of course. He must be, so confident, so powerful. Gabby licked her lips, one hand reaching toward him beneath the table, without her consent, touching the tip of his knee. She watched his pupils dilate, darkness taking over the green, as she smiled.

Gabby, emboldened by his response and her own growing need, touched his glass, taking it suggestively from his lips and tasted it, slowly, her tongue running over the lip of the crystal to catch every drop. "I'm in the company of a great hero, it seems."

"And I of a hero's widow." That didn't seem

to curtail his own desire, much to her delight. To the contrary. Michael leaned forward, his hand, in turn, touching her face, ever so lightly. Her face felt like a magnet being pulled into his open palm, her whole body responding to his touch. Moisture blossomed as she licked the liquor but her nether lips were just as wet. She had no idea she'd been so starved for a man's attention.

"I hope you don't think me too bold." She handed over his glass again, watched him turn it toward him and drink from the exact spot she had, tasting her there. "I would ask a favor, a boon this evening."

"Anything you desire, Gabriella. I will give it to you, if it be in my power." The subtle suggestion was almost enough to push her over the edge. Oh, how delicious this game he agreed to play with her. How tantalizing and engaging, exciting her to new courage.

"I fear those thieves may know where I live and come looking for retribution." A foolish worry. They would never risk attacking her manor house. In fact, she was shocked they'd even made an appearance on her lands at all. "Would you please be so kind and stay the night? Just to keep them at bay, if they are so bold."

And there it was, the offer on the table, while she held her breath and hoped. Rewarded when he smiled ever so faintly, breath catching before he spoke in that deep voice made deeper by desire. "I will keep you safe from them, dear Gabriella, if I, too, may be so bold." He exhaled a shaking breath, hand catching for her cheek, touch firmer this time, hotter. "But I can't say the same for myself if I stay." He pulled against her, tugging her close, lips over hers as he exhaled his words over her quivering mouth. "You are too intoxicating for me to stay true to your honor." She panted softly, feeling herself caught up in the sudden surge of passion his touch inspired. "How could I possibly restrain myself from devouring you?" Michael's green eyes already did so, hand unmoved but she felt as if he were already touching her, consuming her.

CHAPTER TWENTY ONE

*A*nd then she was touching him in return, both of her nimble hands under the table, stroking along the thighs of his breeches, climbing toward his lap, needing a better understanding of what her body desired of him. *"It's not yourself you need to worry about."* Her eager hands finally encountered the bulge and it surged in growth beneath her fingers. Gabby gasped softly, her enthusiasm encouraging his straining manhood to come out and play. Michael's head tilted back, a slow and shaking breath escaping, but doing nothing to stop her from artfully guiding him to grow to his full potential.

Gabby laughed, she couldn't help herself, and when she did Michael returned her gaze, his own grin full of promise. He moved swiftly then, pulling her toward him, leaning in to devour her lips with his. His hot tongue tasted every part of her open and eager mouth. Gabby moaned, wanting that mouth to lick her other lips, to feel his tongue dive deep inside her.

But Michael had other plans, more on his mind than hurrying their encounter too that moment of ecstasy. His free hand lightly caressed the top of her breast before tugging at the lace, freeing enough flesh her already straining flesh leaped free. The cold air washed over her erect nipple, catching her breath, as Michael dipped his head. His lips locked on her aching skin, moving his hot tongue over her exposed breast.

Her moans drove him on, tugging her into his lap, burying his face, rough from the beginning of a beard, against her white skin. That wasn't enough for him, and in a surge of strength he rose, picking her up at the waist and landing her on the table, dishes scattering when he pushed them aside. Her skirt was heavy, bulky, in the way but it was no deterrent, not to her hands that tugged and bunched the thick fabric, jerking it high so she could expose herself to him.

Her hunger was like an animal, eating her

alive. Michael's seemed just as consuming as he stuck his finger in the honey jar next to her hip. Sweet nectar drips off his finger as he brought it to her lips, teasing her a moment, not letting her eat, only allowing the tip of her tongue to sample the golden syrup. She moaned again and, with a groan of his own answering, Michael relented, letting her grasp his hand, taking his finger into her mouth, suckling the sweetness from his flesh.

She couldn't get enough, nibbling and licking and sucking to make sure she got all of it. Michael watched her, his eyes narrow slits, breathing through his parted lips in soft pants, until she was done. And then, in another surge of motion, he pulled her into him with one powerful arm, lifting her cumbersome skirt out of the way. Gabby jerked at her underclothes, freeing them, feeling the silken fabric slide free and hit the floor. Shameless, her legs parted, wide and enthusiastic. He didn't disappoint her.

The same finger that dipped in honey found another pot of sweetness, artfully stroking her clitoris. Gabby cried out when he found it erect and willing to perform for him. It was her turn to throw her head back and just let him do what he wanted with her. His mouth found her neck and she was gone, lost to the sweet oblivion of pleasure.

He explored carefully, thoroughly, rubbing

just inside her hot, swollen inner lips. His finger soaked in her juice, he entered her chamber and applies a soft, swirling pressure to the surface.

That small attention sent a massive quake through her, taking her to the edge of orgasm. He stopped at the last moment, leaving her panting, squirming for more.

"Please, stop teasing me." She knew she sounded nothing like a lady, but she didn't care. "I want you inside me, please."

She didn't expect his reaction. His whole body moved with haste, as if her spoken plea was all he waited for. He freed himself from the ties of his breeches, Gabby helping him pull them away from his hips, only to stare in shock when his massive, swollen and throbbing offering was exposed.

So much bigger than her husband, reminding her of the stallion's cock on the road, needing the mare in heat. When Gabby looked up into Michael's eyes, his were shadowed suddenly, concerned by her reaction.

"I'll take great care, milady," he whispered, as though he'd faced this before. Of course he had.

"No," she said with command and excitement, "you will not." She opened wide and grabbed his waist, pulling him into her. "I want you inside me now."

He hesitated, but she wouldn't allow it, and, at last, as she wrapped her legs around him and forced him to relent, he complied. He was stronger than she, so he managed some control, at least a little at first, watching her reaction. But Gabby pulled desperately at his hips with her legs, panting as her hands guided him inside. Taking her need to heart at last, Michael groaned his desire as he drove deep into her body.

She did fear, in the back of the part of her mind that whispered of worry, he might not fit. But Gabby was too far gone to doubt, to wonder, to allow her concerns to rule when his body was here in hers. With her legs locked behind his hard ass, she rocked with him, in perfect timing, the tip of his massive cock massaging against the sensitive places inside her, increasing her pleasure, while she took further delight in fingering her clitoris. Michael rode her hard, panting over her mouth, thrusting deeper with each forward motion of his hips. He forced her to slow, increasing the sensations within, the feel of all of him growing with each movement. Michael shuddered, pulling out almost completely before driving in again. And again. And again.

It drove Gabby wild.

The wave took her, rode her as Michael rode her, forced her breath to stop, her heart to expand, the heat inside her to crest and blow outward as her entire body rippled with the uncontrollable expansion of her passion. Surely she was about to expire from sheer pleasure. She felt the doubled connection of orgasm fed from her rigid clitoris so hard under her fingers and the deep, engulfing pulsing triggered by his cock. She arched her back against his supporting arm and fell into the endless waves of her body's release.

And then, as she began to come down, his own rhythm increased, crested, his body joining her orgasm.

Gabby kissed him deeply while he exploded inside her, his hips locked against her, grunting passion expended into her both her eager mouths. She tightened her grip on his thighs and squeezed inside, knowing it would enhance his pleasure.

With a final thrust he was done, sagging over her, sitting back into his chair with her still wrapped around him, holding her cradled against him. They remained there, tangled and replete, his heartbeat in her ear, just holding each other.

For the first time, even when her husband was alive, Gabby realized she felt completely satisfied.

I looked up from my computer, laughing out loud, rubbing at the goosebumps on my arms, the aching that had started all over again between my thighs.

Awesome. I had to send this to Jones.

Without thinking about it further, I forwarded the saved document to my friend.

When I sat back, exhaling into the quiet air of my apartment, I felt spent, completely and utterly exhausted. I headed back to bed, surprised to see 2AM in glowing green on the clock. I'd written nonstop for hours. And, for the first time ever I didn't feel the desire to go delete what I'd created.

As satisfied as Gabby felt, I crawled into bed. I half considered grabbing my vibrating muse again for one final good night, but decided against it. Instead, smiling, I knew it would be better to get some sleep so I'd have strength tomorrow to continue Gabby sexy saga.

CHAPTER TWENTY TWO

I jumped out of bed the next morning with the hum of excitement still bouncing around my brain. Coffee seemed unnecessary, but habit made me get it started, just as my phone chimed for attention. I knew full well who was messaging me, anticipating the caller's negativity and weighted guilt, but this time Mom's attitude didn't faze me. I just read her message with a kind of calm I'd never have thought to associate with her.

Sunday dinner, and don't forget, bring a vegetable.

Right, the forced family Sunday dinner ritual. Even Richard and his new wife were invited to the farce that was my mother's attempt at making us all seem normal, respectful and grown up about the state of affairs. As I stared at the screen of my phone, her commanding demand for carrots or something equally benign making my stomach churn nonetheless, I had a thought that made me start.

This wasn't healthy, was it? Well, no, Mick, now that you think about it. The fact your crazy mother invites your cheating ex-husband and his pregnant wife to Sunday dinner on the pretense that she adores him (because she didn't constantly criticize and belittle him when he wasn't around) and wants to keep the "family" together (please, spare me) wasn't healthy, just in case I missed it.

I put my phone down before I could shoot off a rude comment, a bit shocked at my reaction but giggling over the idea I might actually tell my mother where she could shove her vegetables. When I poured my first cup of coffee, my thoughts were already on other things and, determined today I was finally going to tell my mother no to dinner just as soon as I enjoyed some caffeine.

I prepared myself for the shit storm that was about to rain down on me as I dialed her number and waited on her answer. The instant her unhappy voice said, "Hello?" like she knew what I was about to say, I dove in.

"Mom? Hi, sorry but I have plans tonight. I

can't make—"

Before I even finished my sentence, her massive sigh of disapproval drowned me out. But I was ready for it. I continued like she hadn't tried to smother me in guilt. "Hope you understand how uncomfortable it will be for me to be in the same room with Richard and his new wife, especially now that we all know she's pregnant." Mom. Please understand.

Instead, she responded with an even louder sigh, this one in her disgusted tone. "M*ichaela*, you know Richard has been a part of the family *forever*. It's *tradition*." Seriously? I grit my teeth as she plowed on. "What are we without tradition and family gatherings? If I didn't insist we all get together, we would never see each other." I'd give my mother one thing, she was the Queen of Guilt and no one would ever unseat her from that throne. "No, Michaela, I don't except your excuse. You're a grown woman, for goodness sake. Do you really want him to see you as weak?" Like I cared what Richard thought. But I did, I really did, hating it, hating Mom in that moment, but most of all hating myself. "You're expected at 6PM sharp, young lady, and don't forget to bring a vegetable. Please make it a green one."

It wasn't lost on me it was likely the only reason Mom wanted me there was for the entertainment factor. She lived for drama. But the little girl in me that hated to disappoint my mother, who still needed her to say just once that she loved me, was proud of me? She betrayed me in that instant between cutting Mom off and being my own woman and going back to doormat status.

"Fine!" I hung up on her, the only defiance I could muster, despite knowing it would amount to her being even worse later, punishment pending. Even as I threw down the phone and fumed over being bullied by a woman who didn't give a crap about me, obviously. Or the way I felt. So why did I care about her?

The thing was, I then had to anticipate my punishment and, knowing exactly what was about to happen next, I cringed when my phone rang. Guess who was calling? Nope, not Mom, that would be too easy, leaving it between us. Instead, sighing and glaring at the screen flashing at me while the jingling chime told me I was about to be chewed out by my sister, I debated not answering.

Not that it would help. If Mom was the Queen of Guilt, Tara was the Princess of Relentless. She'd call me, text me, email me, leave endless messages for hours until I finally gave in.

Which I did, to the expected and immediate accusation. "Mick, why are you trying to upset Mom? Stop being so selfish and suck it up."

My newfound joy was deflating by the

second, the one-two punch of Mom and Tara sucking the life out of me. For the second time in less than half an hour I ended up saying, "fine," though this time with much less rebellion, and hung up.

I sat at my desk for a long moment, staring at the closed laptop, wondering what was wrong with me. Where had my determination gone, my backbone? Why did I let my mother and sister bully me into being the center of their vicious need to see this mess unfold in front of them like a sick stage play they bought tickets for?

Thing was, I knew dinner would be uncomfortable but quiet. I wouldn't say a thing about the baby, because it was easier to avoid the confrontation, choke down my meal and escape another week.

I flipped open the laptop cover, angry suddenly, needing to escape. I just wanted a few minutes of peace, to recreate some of that spark that ran through my veins not so long ago. Instead, I stared at the screen while doubt rose and whispered in my ear.

Was what I'd written last night any good after all?

I jumped a little, a tiny meep of surprise escaping when my phone chimed again. I almost didn't look, not wanting to read any hateful messages from Mom or Tara, but doing the inevitable dread check anyway. And, to my surprise and surge of tingly passion, recognized Elliot's number.

Had I ever opened a message that fast before in my life?

I'd love to take you for dinner tonight, if you're free.

I collapsed inside, hating my mother all over again. Tonight of all nights. Was I about to lose my only shot with him because of stupid green vegetables and Mom's need for conflict? Hesitant, but knowing I didn't have a choice, I responded.

I'm so sorry. I can't tonight. I have a family thing. I wish I could get out of it.

Dread worse than anything I'd felt before washed over me the instant I hit send. That was it, then. He'd see the rejection and take that as a no thanks and I'd never get another opportunity. My life sucked.

No worries. Figured it was a long shot. What about tomorrow night?

His reply was not only faster than I expected, the words didn't make sense to me for a long time while I finally realized he hadn't dropped me like a hot rock. I said no and he was okay with it. Had this been Richard? He'd have moved on instantly.

The only problem was, as I sat there and thought about Elliot, about my life, about the weight of everything I was dealing with, I accepted defeat. Yes, he was handsome and kind and I was interested. But I just didn't have it in me to do anything about it. How could I when I didn't even have the courage to really, truly stand up to my mother and sister?

Sorry, Elliot, I'm super busy right now. I know your leaving soon and not sure if I'll have time before you go.

I read the horrible betrayal of a message about ten times before I pressed send, all the while talking myself through my excuses. After all, he was leaving soon, so what was the point? Not like we had a shot at anything except maybe a one-night-stand which meant Paul was right about him. And I wasn't that kind of girl, anyway. Imagine him thinking I was easy like that. I actually managed to get to offended while I waited for his reply.

When he didn't respond right away, I pushed open my computer in a huff and started to read what poured out of me the previous night, almost afraid of what I'd find. Was it really any good? My phone's chime made me jump, thinking it was Elliot and nervous to read his message when I realized instead it was Jones whose face flashed on the screen.

HOLY MOTHER OF FUCK, SO GOOD, WHAT HAPPENS NEXT? KEEP GOING!

I couldn't help myself. I did smile a little and that gave me the strength to continue to read what I'd written the night before.

Unfortunately, the first thing that registered wasn't the story, the passion, but the typos, plot holes and errors in the timeline. Mistakes glared from every page as I spent the next fifteen minutes completely ripping it apart.

When I sat back from the remains of what I'd done, I exhaled with my throat tight from pending tears. Keep going, she said. To where? I slammed the laptop closed and gulped for air, clutching at my chest with both hands, fighting off the need to sob my regret and hurt and all the aching pain I'd been living with for so long into the quiet of my empty apartment.

One thing was glaringly apparent as I sat there, tears coursing down my face, utter and complete failure engulfing me in a haze of dark clouds I'd never escape. It was time for me to get real and grow up. I wasn't a writer. I was a hack, a faker, a fraud who could barely rub two words together, let alone complete a book. And publish? Who did I think I was?

The laptop's screen came to life as I opened it again and, with a heaviness pressing down on me like I'd never felt, I selected my writing folder and hit delete on every single word. While the computer hummed and obeyed my command, my love of writing died while my heart shuts down and went cold.

CHAPTER TWENTY THREE

S itting at my Mother's table across from Richard, while his new wife sat in my usual spot, was almost too much to bear. Tara perched on hers right beside her own husband. Bill had always been kind to me, but they wouldn't even let me sit beside him so I could talk to someone. Instead, Chere's constant sneaked peeks with those huge, dark eyes in my direction fed my feeling of isolation, trapped between my sister and my mother. Forever, likely. The thought this endless dinner that only started a few minutes ago would never end was so very intense and immediate I had to gulp a mouthful of too-dry white wine to keep myself from screaming.

Ah, family dinner.

Chere finally beamed at my mother in response to the question I'd missed, though her response made it obvious what had been asked. "Yes, Violet, we are so excited, aren't we, Richard?" She turned that wattage on her delicate face, dark hair a sleek bob of perfection framing her soft skin, to my ex-husband before dimpling at Mom again. "Everything has been perfect, I haven't even been sick."

Mom had to ask about the pregnancy. I knew if I ever commented on her choice she'd tell me it was only polite, after all. "Oh, I was terribly sick with both my girls." Mom's usual complaint, how we'd almost killed her, both of us. While I smothered the obvious snarky comeback because she was my mother, and I didn't wish she'd died. Not really. "I was deathly ill for all of it, the two of them. Michaela herself gave me twenty-four gallstones that couldn't be removed until she was born." Sorry, not sorry. More wine followed the first gulp, the dryness becoming palatable with each deep sip.

"That's horrible." Chere's small hand rose to touch her heart. "You poor thing." What a load of pressure to land in a newly pregnant woman's lap. "I consider myself very lucky, on all fronts really." Again with those dimples. "I mean, we even got pregnant on the first try."

My heart froze, cracked, cascaded into dust while I emptied my glass with dull attention. I thought I couldn't get any more numb. I was wrong.

There wasn't enough air at the table. I stood up and started for the kitchen without comment, my glass still in my hand, though empty, to my disappointment. The one upside? I wasn't in the mood to be influenced by my mother's displeasure, her sharp, "Michaela, we're eating!" utterly unworthy of a response or even a shred of care as I slipped through the swinging door and leaned against the counter, breathing slowly and steadily through my mouth. Because if I didn't focus on those deep, even breaths I'd be screaming and throwing things. Mostly at Richard for lying to me yet again.

They got pregnant on the first try. Because she'd tricked him into it.

The bastard.

I only notice then the sounds in the dining room have gone quiet, and I register that silence simply because of its weight. A moment later, Richard entered the kitchen, face tight in a frown, hands extended.

"Michaela, please," like he deserved my forgiveness or even another instant of trust and empathy, "I know this must be tough." Did he? Did he really? I almost laughed. Did Richard have any idea just how huge a farce this whole dinner was? I woke up, like the sun had just blazed to life in my head, the brilliance of it driving out shadows, making everything so clear and sharp it was almost painful to listen to him speak. But I did, standing there, absorbing just how pathetic he really was, and how equally ridiculous I'd been letting this whole mess play out without a fight. "This isn't what you think."

I did laugh then, a hearty mix of real joy and bitterness. "Yes," I said. "Yes, it is."

He closed the distance slowly like I was some kind of wild animal he needed to calm before he could put me out of my misery. I was trapped between lies and the sink, but for once I saw through the former and the latter was doing a great job keeping me from punching him in the face.

"No, you have to understand. This isn't how it happened." Nothing he said was true. In that instant of clarity I saw his lies like colored bubbles, balloons tainted with oozing blackness that turned him from a handsome prince into the worst kind of freak show. "I told you she planned it. I had no idea." He took that last step, fingers locking on my elbow, his attempt at a human expression of pleading and remorse a caricature of what truth really was. "Michaela, I would never hurt you like this."

I didn't mean to cry. I wasn't weeping for him, not for what he said, the obviousness now of the lies he told. No, I was crying for release, as I'd orgasmed the night before, letting out something I'd held onto for far too long. And while I hated that I'd come here tonight, I felt a flexing of gratitude that I could finally see him for who he really was.

"Just go back to dinner, Richard." I shook off his hand and shrugged. "I'll be fine."

He smiled like my words meant more than the tears streaming down my face. "You're the best, Mick. You always were." He turned and left me there as if that solved everything, fixed the mess he'd made of my life.

No, not him. Me. I gulped air and nodded into the empty room, to myself. My responsibility. I'd allowed this disaster, allowed these ungrateful, hateful people into my life, a continuing place in my life. Was this all I deserved? Someone in the other room laughed. Sounded like Tara. *Laughed.* That sound cut through me, to the bone, the core of me, leaving me to bleed more tears as I realized not one of the others would make an attempt, take even a heartbeat to check on me, to make sure I was all right.

Was this what other people's families did to each other? Or were we really that special?

I don't remember when I chose to just leave. It happened organically, an unconscious act that found me striding out the kitchen door into the living room, past the opening to the dining room where the others gaped as I walked out. Despite her usual protests, not even Mom tried to stop me.

Perfect exit. Richard and Chere should have gotten pregnant ages ago. I choked on that, pushed past it as I closed the door behind me. I rested my back against the frame for three heartbeats, gathering my strength, listening to another round of laughter from inside the apartment. Wiped the last of the tears from my face. And left that hateful place behind.

My walk to the station passed without my knowledge, my firm steps carrying me on autopilot to board the train, take a seat. I knew I'd break sooner or later, that my heart and mind were protecting me until I was safe and I was okay with that. My apartment called and I could curl up under the covers, drown in a hailstorm of chips and chocolate while letting the shattered remains of who I was shrivel to nothing.

That's why I was so shocked with myself when I started to cry. So not like me to let go in public. It was a battle, then, to try to not let go of control and sob where everyone would see me despite needing it so very much.

By the time I exited the train my coat cuffs were soaked through with the continuing leak of tears. I knew I had to look a wreck because I felt worse and, when I paused to look in a window at my reflection, I hated the red-cheeked, hollow-eyed woman staring back at me. She'd betrayed me most of all, sending me into that den of hatred with barely a fight to be had.

I spotted the neon sign up ahead, the bar beckoning, and without a moment of hesitation headed right for the door to Tally's. This time any man who came near me would be at threat to his life and limb because I was about to drown my sorrows until I couldn't remember a thing.

I sat at the bar and ordered a double whiskey. If the bartender recognized me he didn't say so, though he did eye me with raised eyebrows.

"You all right, miss?" His kindness was unexpected. At first look, the night I'd first come in here, all I'd seen was chiseled, tattooed arms, a bearded, closed off face and a ratty t-shirt over jeans that likely had holes in the knees. He looked like the kind you would see in a bar fight, not concerned over someone like me. My eyes welled once more, but I waved my hand at him and ducked my head to hide it.

"I'm fine, thank you. Just the drink." End of story. I just couldn't handle the stereotypical bartender therapist thing at that moment.

He didn't comment, the glass containing my order sliding over the bar to my waiting hand a few seconds later while I did my best to just sink into the surface of the amber liquid. At least Sunday night didn't attract a huge crowd, so if I was going to embarrass myself again, at least I wouldn't have many witnesses.

Poured steadily over the gulped glass of wine, the Scotch quickly did its duty on me, my body relaxing and my mind slowing down. I was surprised to find the world wavered when I looked up and tried a smile. "Can I please have a refill, sir?" So polite, Mick.

"I'll take care of that." I turned a bit too quickly at the sound of that familiar voice, wobbling on my stool, catching myself, but not before Paul's hands did, too. He grinned at me, settling me but not releasing me, one hand drifting down my arm to settle on my knee, bare under the raised hem of my skirt. "Hey, Mick." He was so close to me I could smell the beer on his breath mixed with that garlic scent that churned my stomach. "Funny to find you here on a Sunday."

"Bad day." It was the best I had to offer.

Paul's demeanor changed, almost kind suddenly, to my surprise. His other hand released his drink again and rubbed my back, the one on my knee flexing. It actually felt rather good, though I sipped my drink and wondered if it was just because it had been so long since someone touched me.

"Sorry to hear that, kid," he said. "Tell old Paul all about it. I'm a great listener."

I downed my second double and raised my hand to the bartender. "One more, please." He actually hesitated, glancing at Paul, then back to me. What? With a shrug, he free poured a measure of whiskey into my glass and turned his back.

Paul, meanwhile, kept rubbing, rubbing, his other hand traveling slowly up my leg while I observed that touch with distant curiosity. Wow, I was drunk already. Imagine that. "I don't think I've ever seen you like this." He leaned in and his lips brushed against my temple. Or did I imagine it? "I'm here for you, Mick. I've always been here for you."

"Have you ever had your whole world just implode right before your eyes?" I think I said that. I meant to say that. But I wasn't exactly fully coherent anymore. How odd to be so disconnected from what my mind wanted and what my body could deliver. This was worse than the other night. I'd gone over the tipping point and observed it from a distance, like I wasn't in my body anymore but hovering, watching the girl at the bar drink too much while her coworker touched her inappropriately. "I need to change it up, Paul. That's what I need to do. I can't keep doing what I've been doing."

He nodded like I was making sense, and maybe I was. Whatever. I had reached the point where my whole spirit felt anesthetized and when he answers I can't process what he's saying. And while a part of me really wanted him to leave me alone and was sickened by his obviousness, I leaned into him because I just miss having a body beside me.

I needed to get up, to go. When I tried, I slipped, knees buckling, Paul catching me.

"Whoa there, little lady, let me help you." I let him, waving off the bartender who watches us as we go, Paul a gentlemen as he guided me toward the bathrooms. No, I needed to leave, but he was right, his instincts were good. I was going to throw up and I didn't want to do that on the street, did I?

Part of my nausea came from being so close to him. The scent of yeasty beer and cologne, the faint undertone of his personal garlic musk, all combined to raise my bile, though if I was sober it likely wouldn't have triggered my disgust. I looked up as he stopped at the bathroom door, and impulsively reach up to run my hand over his face.

Paul lit up, eyes huge, teeth bared in a smile, leaning in to kiss me. And, in that moment of weakness and longing, of hurt and despair, I found myself past the point of caring. I wanted to feel something, anything. And when he pivoted me sideways and gave me a bit of a shove, I let him, passing instead through the door to the men's room.

How did we get into a stall, the door still

gaping open, his hands everywhere, his mouth clamped over mine while I fought for breath I couldn't catch? I tasted his hot saliva, the roughness of his teeth clamping on my lower lip, the harsh grasp of his hands tugging at my skirt. My back ached instantly from the awkward position as he sat me on the toilet tank, jerking on his belt, his button and zipper while I froze, still and empty and unwilling to stop him despite knowing this was wrong, a mistake.

His pants hit the floor, underwear to his knees as he pushed himself between my legs. His mouth gnawed my neck, an animal in heat, hands fighting my underwear while I inhaled and exhaled. "No."

Paul's whole body jerked, practically leaped away from mine. He listened, he knew what no meant. But in that instant I realized my error. Not his choice. No, it was the towering, furious Elliot who'd made that decision for all of us.

CHAPTER TWENTY FOUR

"Are you ok? Do you need help?" Nice of him to ask after he'd pulled Paul away from me and sent him careening into the flimsy wall of the bathroom stall. Elliot's concern was a weight on my chest while I clumsily and hastily tugged down my skirt, slipping when I tried to step off the back of the toilet. Made worse when his big hands helped me even though I wanted to crawl under a rock.

"What the...?" Paul jerked his pants up, glaring back and forth between me and Elliot. "Why don't you mind your own business." He reached out to pull me against him, likely to prove some manly point I didn't get, while I fought the urge to throw up all over again.

Elliot ignored him. "Mickey." He didn't sound angry, exactly, or maybe I misheard because I was drunk but in that weird sober feeling zone you get when you've suffered a big shock while under the influence. Everything seemed super sharp and crystal clear despite the spinning the world was trying to do around me. "Would you like me to walk you home?"

I did my best to smooth my clothes, one hand touching my hair, knowing despite doing my best to not look drunk I was making it worse. Humiliation forced me to move, pushing past Paul and Elliot both, not speaking because I knew I'd slur my words, just needing to get out of there.

I was outside in the cool air before I knew I'd left the bar, inhaling and exhaling to keep from puking up the alcohol I'd drunk too fast. Could this night get any worse? I felt the ache of tears, knew there was nothing I could do in my present state and just let myself break down. Pedestrians passed me, a few staring, but I didn't care. Instead, I stood there on the dirty sidewalk with my clothes likely still askew and my head spinning, my heart wanting to abandon me utterly, sobbing my heart out.

My body wanted a good wailing session from the beginning, way before tonight, before hearing about the pregnancy, before I found out Richard had cheated on me. I'd needed to grieve for all the children I could have had, mourning them as if not giving them an option to be conceived was worse than letting Richard manipulate me into not being a mother. They didn't even get a chance to *be*.

I started walking, wobbling, heading for my stoop up ahead, keeping my eyes locked on it despite the wavering vision through the haze of tears and whiskey, focusing on that destination with all my strength. Not that I cared about my neighbors or the passing people. This wasn't about anyone but me and my grief. I'd never experienced something so all-consuming before and honestly, drunk or not, I'm positive I would have ended up the same way.

I let it out all the way to the steps, inside my building, to my floor, through my front door while Mrs. Barrow peeked into the hall with that characteristic scowl on her face. I ignored her and slammed my door, hating my life, my job, my marriage which I should have ended years ago when he didn't want children. It was all my fault. I'd wasted my life on a lie and now what did I have? Even that dream that kept me going, the creative birthing of words on the page, had abandoned me. I thought I could actually be a writer.

How delusional. Why would that work out for me, either?

I landed hard on my sofa, head back, spinning growing worse as I groaned and remembered my latest humiliation. Thank god Elliot walked in when he did, or I might have done the unthinkable with Paul, despite saying no.

Oh. God. *Elliot.* I sat upright, too fast, gulped and ran for the kitchen sink, knowing I'd never make it to the bathroom. Tonight's feeble attempt at a few bites of dinner and a whole lot of booze poured out of me as I heaved, not just out of physical need, but emotional shame and regret. By the time I was done, coughing and rinsing my mouth, I actually felt better, at least enough to stagger back to the couch and hug a big, soft pillow for comfort.

Which only made me think of Elliot again. He'd walked in and seen everything. That thought replayed over and over in my mind. Completely devastated but finally spent, I sighed about it, filed it under write offs I'd accumulated in my life and accepted I'd made a massive disaster out of a nice little mess.

My phone buzzed in my purse and I fished it out, barely enough energy to swipe right.

Are you okay, Mickey?

Elliot's kindness was too much. He really needed to get the hint I wasn't the kind of girl he should be trying to save. Instead of answering, I turned my phone off.

No more messages. Not the one from my mother waiting for me to check it, or from Tara, or even from Richard. Nope. I was so done. Wishing I could rewind my night—my life, thanks—I hauled myself to bed.

The alarm blared at 6AM, jerking me upright to groan and clutch my aching head. Bright red numbers glared accusingly, like they tried to warn me Monday morning was coming, I just didn't listen. I felt like I had been thrown out of a moving bus doing 80MPH on the highway.

I staggered to the bathroom, wincing at my reflection in the mirror, not wanting to meet my own eyes while my head threatened to implode. I considered calling in sick, leaning against the sink, shaking hand wiping at the cold sweat on my forehead.

Don't you dare.

My mother berated me without even having to be there. Lovely. Fine. I'd face the music, Paul and, ultimately, Elliot, hung over or not.

I managed to sneak into the office despite being five minutes late and look busy enough no one bothered me or questioned my timing. A couple of painkillers and a giant bottle of water nursed me far enough into health I was able to throw myself into my work and ignore everyone around me. As the first hour passed, Paul behind me at his own cubicle not even trying to say hello, I resolved to purge the night before from my memory.

Or, tried to. Paul finally wheeled over to my desk, leaned into me, hand touching my knee while he pretended to look at my screen. Acting like this was appropriate behavior. A massive surge of disgust and revulsion hit me hard between my shoulder blades, unexpected, violent, as I pushed his hand away.

He looked startled, then winked like I hadn't just pretty much told him to piss off. "Just having a little look-see," he smirked. Paired then with a knowing wink, to my despair. "I'd like to get an even better look, next time," he said, voice dropping low, eyebrows waggling at me, his hand running the length of my upper arm.

I gaped at him, stunned. Was he cracked? I struggled to form a coherent *hell no*, never in a million years when he leaned in to kiss me.

My chair's wheels skittered over the carpet as I pushed him back, mortified to my core. "Paul, we're at work." I meant to say more, to deny him utterly, instead knowing I'd only made things worse. Instead of saying no, I'd suggested outside work might still be okay. Hadn't I? I was so confused, heart fluttering with denial and embarrassment, I felt my cheeks heat, my whole body poised to rise and run away. Naturally, the eyes of everyone in the office were looking at us. Judging, assuming.

Please, whatever powers that be were out there, just let me die.

Paul winked, shrugged. "You loved it last night." He backed off then, wheeling to his desk and leaving me alone while I stared anywhere but at him. Meeting Lauren's disapproving glare. I forced myself to slowly look around at the others as they shifted their uncomfortable gazes so quickly some could have given themselves whiplash. It was only then I realized it wasn't Paul's attempted display that had everyone staring.

Oh. My. God. He'd told everyone what happened last night. All I could do was put my head down and work. Get through it somehow. After all, some other gossip worthy event would eventually come up and everyone would talk about that. Thing was, I was always on the other side and being in the thick of office gossip? I knew exactly what was being said about me.

I was going to have to leave the country. Maybe the planet. Were they still looking for volunteers to go to Mars? I'd heard it was going to be a one-way trip. My luck, I'd get rejected. I'd lost my freaking mind somewhere along the way and had no idea how to get it back.

Trying to go anywhere in the office was a hassle all day because Paul was right there, waiting to follow me, hoping for a playback from the night before, more than likely. Staff room, bathroom, you name it, he was there, lurking, trying to make small talk, to corner me so he could touch me. I'd never felt so vulnerable in my life and, finally, knew I had to say something to Judy.

Which meant admitting to Judy I'd made a horrible mistake. That drove me back to my desk without saying a word. Damn, I hated this place. It was a huge realization, one that hit me as I stared into the computer screen, trapped by this project with Paul, by my own inability to act.

Elliot had to choose that moment, when I was at my lowest, to walk around the corner into the office. I ducked my head, unable to meet his eyes, and was relieved when he kept his distance, joining Judy behind her door.

Almost on cue, Richard's number popped up on my phone, a desperate text following.

Please, can you help me?

Honestly, I almost ignored it this time, except for the fact Paul had turned toward me, was looking right at me like he was going to make another move. Anything would be better than having to face another moment of this. I glanced at the clock, lunchtime close enough I could make a break for it, diving for my purse and heading for the elevator. I could feel Paul staring, an itch forming between my shoulder blades, but when I strode onto the elevator

with a handful of others, I turned to find he hadn't followed. Even as I texted Richard back.
  Be right there.

CHAPTER TWENTY FIVE

I knocked on Richard's apartment door, wondering what I was thinking. Yes, I'd used him as an excuse to get out of work, to escape Paul and humiliation, but I hadn't actually intended to follow through. Except, here I was, like always, making myself available when he had never, ever been.

The door opened to the lovely Chere, short, shiny dark hair in a bob, makeup so precise it was professional, as I remembered grappling with Paul while drunk in the bar bathroom wasn't the only embarrassing thing that happened to me last night. How had I forgotten walking out of Mom's with my tail between my legs?

My eyes dropped to her protruding belly, draped artfully in graceful, white lace dress. The tablet was in her hand but I couldn't make my own rise to accept it, not when she watched me carefully, like I was a wild animal she wasn't sure was safe to be around. Punctuated by her free hand sliding over the curve of the child inside her, protective. I registered the scent of lavender, the warmth of sunshine on the hardwood floors behind her. Odd to take in such details when my heart was breaking all over again.

"Richard called," she said, sounding uncertain but smiling, forced and tight. "So nice of you to help, Mickey."

I accepted the tablet but didn't move, knowing I had to leave, to just get out of there before I said or did something I'd regret further. Except I couldn't, not without asking the question I knew would end everything for me for good.

"You've been planning this for a while." It didn't come out as a question, though, but a statement. I gesture vaguely at her pregnancy.

She nodded, both hands now covering the bump under the dress. "Yes, for months. We even thought we might have to try IVF, but it worked out. So far so good."

I nodded, mouth watering, the need to throw up rising in the back of my throat, more powerful even than last night when I had alcohol as an excuse. "IVF is expensive." Mick, what a thing to say.

But Chere laughed a little, startled, and eye rolled. "I know. Richard wanted to spare no expense, though. He knows how much having children means to me."

She might as well have slammed the door in my face. Did she understand what she'd just done to me, in that innocent moment of conversation between women who'd shared the man who loved her more than he ever loved me? That much was clear as I bobbed a nod, managed a smile.

"Congratulations." I turned and walked away, chest heavy, tablet a fifty-pound brick in my hands, not even acknowledging her calling my name as I left.

It wasn't like I really needed confirmation he'd been lying to me all along. More importantly, really, was the flaw in my own character. How had I even thought there was a scrap of good in him? I stared down at his tablet in my hands as the elevator let me out on the ground floor and the city opened up before me past the exit into the street. Normally I would have been planning out what I was going to say to Richard, my interaction with him spinning out in my head over and over before I even got to him. Instead, today, I felt numb, blank.

This would be the last time. And I didn't

even have the energy to tell him why.

My phone buzzed as I headed for the subway, Judy's number catching my attention. *Need you at 386 Maylor. Mr. Pekette needs budget breakdown explanation in person.*

Richard's tablet slipped quietly and without complaint into my purse as I shrugged off that errand and changed directions. He could wait.

The renovation looked like a bomb site as I stepped over a pile of discarded drywall and joined the short, balding man whose red cheeks and frustration were so visible I almost turned around and walked away. I really wasn't in any mood to be gracious or kind today, but Mr. Pekette spotted me and waved me over. We'd met once before, so I knew he recognized me and, the moment he opened his mouth, I was battered with the small man's frustration and attitude.

"Do you see this?" He waved both arms over his head, almost like a cartoon character prepping to explode primary colors all over the decimation of his downstairs foyer. "This is a disaster! I've spent over $200,000 already, for what? This mess? What am I supposed to do with this mess, Miss O'Keefe?" My breath caught at the last name I still used, that more a betrayal to myself than anything else. I really had to shed Richard's identity. Meanwhile Mr. Pekette's voice rose in volume, mottled red now climbing down his neck into the white collar of his suit. "You're already at budget with this project and all I have is a giant mess!"

Defining moments in life happen when you least expect them, don't they? Maybe if it had been just Mr. Pekette's freak out I could have managed. Maybe. But, right on cue, as the small man's temper hit me like a freight train over something that wasn't my fault, my phone buzzed. I fished it out of my bag, hoping it was Judy, that I could pass this furious little man on to my boss, only to see an angry message from Richard.

Where is my tablet? You know I need it. Hurry up.

"Are you listening to me?" Mr. Pekette's temper wasn't getting any better. I looked up from my phone, into his furious eyes, and felt myself twitch.

"I'll be right with you." His eyes bulged at my tone while I typed a message back to the biggest dick in my life. *I'll be there when I get there.* I had only just hit send when, vibrating with rage, Mr. Pekette reached out and grabbed my phone from my hand.

I gaped at him as he waved it in the air above his head, almost dancing in his fit of utter frustration. "How dare you brush me off for another client? I want answers, and if you don't give them to me I'm suing your company."

I felt the snap of the fraying elastic band

barely holding me together just finally let go. I'd dealt with my mother, my sister, Richard, the baby. Paul telling the office we were together, or at least sleeping together. Elliot being nice, too nice, while my life fell apart. While this arrogant little turd had the nerve to threaten me over a job I'd just come to understand I hated. With a passion.

"You overbearing, bullying asshole." I heard myself talking, knew words were coming out of my mouth, but I had zero control over them or the tone of delivery, for that matter. A massive wave of something that felt like relieved giddiness rose with my retort, even as a tiny part of me cringed that there would be fallout. Didn't matter in the moment, not when I was riding that wave toward what seemed like personal redemption. "How dare you treat me like crap over something that isn't my fault? You want to sue, go for it. Sue. Like I give a sweet flying rat's ass about your project at this moment, with that attitude." Oh, Mickey.

I'd never seen anyone that close to a stroke before. He gurgled while I grabbed my phone back from his now limp hands and shrugged before turning and storming out.

The second I hit the pavement remorse and terror took over. I had to call Judy, to tell her what happened. She'd side with me, surely. The man was unreasonable, going ballistic on me like that. My phone buzzed angrily and I glanced at Richard's string of furious responses while that rebellious part of me slammed into my chest once again and took hold before I could call my boss and tell her what happened.

I stood at a crossroads, that much was certain. With Richard and maybe with my whole life. I reached into my purse and fished out the tablet, staring down at it like I'd never seen it before. Why was I clenching it so hard my fingers were numb and white? I glanced sideways at the dumpster outside the Pekette residence, high sides looming over me. And, in that instant, my new and fed up Mickey made a choice that would change everything.

With a perfectly executed toss, I underhanded the tablet up over the edge of the dumpster, the leather case dull in the sunlight as it arched beautifully in slow motion before plunging into the trash where it belonged.

No regret woke. Huh, imagine that. I wiped my hands together like they were dirty or something, before rubbing them on my thighs for good measure. I hesitated, knowing I really needed to go back to see the client, to apologize and fix things before calling Judy, but I just didn't want to.

Was this what a nervous breakdown felt like?

Inhaling city air, I started walking to nowhere in particular. Head up, clear minded and oddly lighthearted, I found myself smiling as I went. Big change from last night. I had forgotten how much I loved my city, the architecture, the steady hum of activity. Growing up here, I'd always thought it was the best place on earth.

I found my way underground and boarded the subway, letting the train take me wherever it was going. Indifference was a new sensation for me, liquid and lucid but without emotion. I just let go and went with the flow, enjoying for the first time the feeling of absolutely nothing. It was almost like a meditative state, something I'd never been able to accomplish, not with my mind running, telling me I was doing it wrong.

When I reached the end of the line, I left the train and climbed to the surface, turning left at random and started walking. I finally found myself standing on a grassy verge, a small park peaceful and empty before me, a bench beckoning. I drifted to it, sat down, inhaled fresher air than downtown and tucked my cold hands in my pockets, enjoying the fading sunlight. I shed my shoes despite the October chill and let the grass comfort my toes.

I don't know how long I sat there, feeling nothing. Until I discovered I was crying silently, moisture dripping down to land in my lap. Tears were becoming good friends to me.

I know you're going through something. I read the text message that made my phone buzz, only because it was from Elliot and he was the only one who seemed to be able to get a rise in emotion from me at the moment. Shocked to find he was texting me at all. Why hadn't he written me off by now? *I've been there.* Sure he had. Wait, he said he had, didn't he? Something about hating his life, too, once upon a time. I read on. *I'd really like to take you to dinner. To talk. If you'll let me.*

I stared down at that chance to connect and almost rejected it. But the unfeeling moment was passing, the lightness and clarity receding in favor of real regret, faint panic. I wiped at the tears and messaged him back.

Let's meet right now.

CHAPTER TWENTY SIX

"That was *not* me Elliot, I don't know what I was thinking." The second I sat down with the handsome photographer my mouth started running and it hadn't stopped yet. Funny how the excuses started to pile up after a while. "I'm not used to drinking so much either, I'm a mess. And I'm so embarrassed. I mean Paul? Please believe me that was a completely different person. I just lost my mind sitting at that dinner table, listening to everyone talking about their lives like they didn't know mine was falling apart." Elliot's silence encouraged me to continue, as did his compassionate expression, his slow nodding. "I need to make a change. This isn't working, Richard and Chere at my mother's for every Sunday dinner. Seriously? Who does that?" I finally sagged in my seat, sipping at my water to ease my parched throat, realizing I'd spent the last fifteen minutes dumping the rest of my crap on him, that all I'd seemed to do with Elliot was shed unhappiness into his lap. I hung my head, suddenly wishing I was anywhere but here.

"Mick." I looked up, expecting rejection, meeting only kindness and flinching from it. "If you don't mind some advice?" I nodded then. What was weird? I fully expected him to tell me to get a life, to berate me and punish me for my failings. Anticipated it with something akin to eagerness even as he exhaled and offered a small, sad smile. "You are the only person in this equation that matters." Wait, what? Where was the get your shit together, Mickey, what's wrong with you anyway? Elliot wasn't playing by the same script I had running in my head. "You and only you are important. What you want for you." Was I open-mouthed in shock? But wait, he wasn't the only person who'd said things like this to me, was he? Jones. He sounded like Jones.

Elliot leaned forward and touched my hand, fingers sliding around mine, gripping them gently, the warmth of his skin cancelling out the chill from the cold glass I'd just held in a flare of heat. "It's time to be selfish and do what you want. Not what you think other's want you to do to make them feel better."

I shook my head, trying to comprehend what he was saying. Selfish? They were the selfish ones. I couldn't be like that, act like that. But he wasn't done.

"What I say, your mother, your boss..." Elliot let me go, leaning on his elbows, eyes intense as they held me in place. "No one gets a say, Mick. Only you. So, I ask you, who do you want to be? What do you really want to do? And how do you get it?"

A spark of hope woke, fluttered around my heart as his words got through, even as I sagged, wondering who this man was, what he'd been smoking before he came to meet me. I fought off the familiar sting in my eyes, the tightness in my throat. I would not cry my way through this conversation. Instead, I found myself clinging to what he said, protecting it like my life depended on it.

Weird, I was actually hungry. I helped myself to the guacamole and chips he'd ordered, as he continued.

"If you don't mind me asking, where your dad is in all this?" Elliot took a generous mouthful of deliciousness that had nothing to do with the food in front of us. Was I really still hot for him after everything I'd been through? Yes, yes I was.

"My mom would say he lives under a bridge or something, like the troll she says he is." I'd grown up with that imagery in my head. "She doesn't think too highly of him. But, to tell you the truth, I can see why he left." Of course I could. Mom was a nightmare. "She's controlling." Understatement. "I can imagine a life with her as a partner." I shook my head. "No, not a partner. It wouldn't even be that. He was her employee." I took a sip of water. "I really don't know why the both of them are so mean." I'd switched gears on him again, bringing my sister into it without warning. "What happened to make them so hateful? I feel it sometimes, what they really think about me." I hadn't meant to say that. It escaped in a soft exhale. "I'm surprised I didn't end up like them. Maybe Jones has something to do with it." Jones. Where was she? I needed her and yet, I had Elliot. The sensation of emotionless hovered at the edges of me, but he held it at bay, kept me from either flying off the deep end into begging Richard and Judy for forgiveness, crawling back to Mom and Tara or walking off the pier and letting go utterly. "As for your question, I haven't seen my dad since I was six."

Elliot must have known my mind was wandering. "Have you ever thought about looking him up? See what kind of man he really is? Not taking someone else's account of who he might be? Rebuilding your sense of family with someone new?" Elliot smiled and reached across the table once again, squeezing my hand, light and quick before he pulled back once more, face still beaming at me. That spark of hope grew a little bit more. "And what about this famous Jones you talk about? When did you meet?"

I laughed out loud, thinking of our first encounter. "We were in elementary school, recess. There was this massive snow pile. All the kids were trying to run to the top and some boy, I can't remember his name, pushed me down so he could get up first." I could almost feel the snow, hear the boy's jeering taunts. "All of a sudden this girl flew over me. She grabbed the boy's hood and dragged him to the bottom of the hill, pushing his face in the dirty snow." Jones had looked up at me with a broad smile, cheeks pink. "She made him apologize. We've been besties ever since."

"She sounds great," he said, his eyes never changing, still kind, open, understanding. "Another person to call family." What did he mean, exactly? What did Dad and Jones have to do with anything?

He was getting to that, it turned out. "I understand what you're going through, more than you know. I told you I was married for fifteen years. At first, it was fun and carefree, then our lives became about work and making money. She became distant and I knew, even though I wouldn't admit it to myself. I knew she was gone way before we made it official. The hardest part was showing up at my best friend's house and her car was in his driveway. I sat there for hours, completely numb. Afraid to go inside but knowing I needed to, just as my friend came out the front door and walked toward me." Elliot's turn to sip water, though he sounded less overwhelmed and just thoughtful. Had he found his way through the grief of it? Weird how it felt so intimate and yet like a story, nothing more. "He seemed so casual about it. I was shaking. I didn't know what I was going to do when he asked me to come inside. They didn't even try and hide it. They told me they loved each other and she was leaving. They were supposed to be the two people that had my back. At that moment I knew I was the only one to make me feel anything. I tried to make her happy and she just got more frustrated and angry with me. It was really hell on earth." He shrugged. "I'd made the wrong choices, tried to cling to the two people who I thought could give me what I needed. Only to have them betray me."

I was beginning to understand what he was talking about. "So you walked away from both of them. Found new family to trust?"

He shook his head, but instead of explaining, finished his story. "Right now at this moment, I can say I'm so grateful to both of them. I really am." That was in defense of my instinctual reaction of disbelief I know flashed over my face. "I thank them every day because I got my head out of my ass and made real changes. The kind that makes me jump out of bed in the morning." Elliot toyed with a forkful of guacamole. "I can say with 100% certainty I would never have asked to separate, so I would have been sentenced forever to a loveless, hateful situation of a shell of who I wanted to be." He raised his eyebrows at me. "Can you see that?"

I subconsciously picked up a chip and dipped into the green mix before sticking it my mouth while he continued.

"I quit my job, bought a DSL camera and started to take photographs, and haven't looked back." He laughed suddenly, a light and joyful sound that made me stop chewing, stop everything, and just stare at him. "That was eight years ago and, seriously, every morning when I wake up I smile and say thank you."

"Okay, I get that," I said. "It worked for you, that's great." What was I going to do? Quit my job and write books no one would read even if I managed to finally finish one? And looking up Dad, whatever. Not to mention relying on Jones. I couldn't even get her to call me back and I needed her so much right now.

Elliot's   smile   faded   to   gentle

understanding. "It can work for you, too. You just need the right people to lean on until you figure out where you want to go from here."

"Where did *you* go first?" I admitted I was curious, even if what he was saying was totally unrealistic.

"Colombia," he said, while fear woke and said, "Nope!" But Elliot's big smile was back. "It was the first place I thought of. Mickey, it was amazing. The people, the culture, the natural beauty. At that time its people and their land were being ravaged by warring cartels, but it was worth the danger. I ended up getting some amazing shots that a couple of big nature magazines bought and my new career was born."

I swallowed my bite of appetizer, feeling a mix of that woken hope and a little ill from fear. Elliot's gaze had turned intense and he ignored the food while he asked his next question.

"What about you, Mickey? What does your deepest desire want you to do? What do you want?"

I already knew what I wanted, despite myself, despite my failures, the call of the keyboard undeniable. I almost said it, even though I'd deleted all of the files I'd saved off my laptop. A writer. I wanted to tell stories for a living. I stared at my hands as I fought to answer, knowing this wasn't for him, not to impress him or anyone else, not to pretend to be but to commit to being, for me.

Elliot went on first. "The moment I met you, I felt your distress." He did? "I saw you in me. It wasn't very pretty my first couple months on my own, Mick. Don't think for a second it was. I'm not making light of this or saying it's a quick fix. Except it is, ultimately. But taking that first step is terrifying, no matter how ready you are." He stared down at his hands now folded on the table in front of him, voice low and quiet. "I had to reprogram my brain to accept I was only doing what I wanted, when I wanted. It was hard to let go of expectations, other people's needs and demands. But it has been so worth the journey."

I couldn't find words to respond, feeling a bit like a tiny child being told life wasn't fair but I could be and do anything I wanted if I really tried.

"Listen," he said, "everyone's journey is their own. Sometimes we need to do something crazy, just to free us from our bondage." He laughed out loud then, catching the attention of fellow diners, but ignored them in favor of me. "Someday I'll tell you some of the insane things I did to just feel something, anything." The sensation of emptiness, of lack of feeling. Had he lived it, too? "I want you to know I'm really attracted to you." And just like that, the conversation shifted and heat rose between us. I sat up straighter in my chair, wondering where this was going suddenly, body craving him in a flare of need so powerful I caught my breath. "Under different circumstances, I would love to get to know you better in a more intimate setting."

Me too. Except I felt the "but" in his words and struggled against tears again while he smiled bigger than the sun.

"That's not what you need right now. I'm not what you need, not sexually. You need to find you way, Mick, and you're just too vulnerable for me to put you in that position."

I hated that I spoke up. "What do I do now?"

He shrugged, pushing the guacamole toward me. "Eat," he said. "And sort the rest out later."

I was tempted to prod him for more, but our main courses arrived and, despite myself, I enjoyed my meal with him. Instead of the depth of conversation we'd been having Elliot kept things light, entertaining me with stories from his time working abroad, kindness and compassion ever present until, when we were finished and ready to leave, I actually felt better than I ever had.

Yes, I had problems, things to sort out. And I would. I had options, support. People who really cared about me. Hope lived, and I embraced it.

When we stood outside the restaurant in the early evening, the cool turned cold, Elliot casually and comfortably leaned in, warm lips pressing softly to my cheek. "Thank you for your company." Wait, he was saying goodbye? Desperate panic came over me and I clutched at his arm through the sleeve of his coat, suddenly terrified. The memory of today, of Richard and the client I'd told off, of Paul and the fact I had played hooky from work all afternoon in an odd state of rebellion so far from my normal took me in a wave of panic. Besides, despite what Elliot said, no matter his supportive stories and his own history, I had no idea what to do from here, where to go. I needed him to tell me.

Did he know? He must have. His kindness never wavered. "It was a pleasure, and don't you dare lose my number. Call me anytime. Don't hesitate. Deal?"

So, leaving me, but staying in my life, if I could believe him. And how could I not believe he wanted me to stay in touch? His demeanor was addictive.

"I won't, and I will." I laughed then, wiped at a stray tear that escaped. "Thank you, Elliot."

We parted ways then, Elliot climbing in a cab on his way to a photo shoot, me walking the three blocks to my apartment with my heart light, fear trying to force me to turn back and hide in the woman I'd been. But I realized as I climbed the steps to my place, there was no going back. Something fundamental had shifted in me since this morning. Since last night. And I didn't want to go back.

I grabbed my phone as I approached my door, remembering I turned it off hours ago, when I sat down to dinner with Elliot, taking a deep breath and feeling inside I was going to be just fine. My screen woke, flashed that I had five messages and two phone calls missed. I slipped into my apartment before reading the first three, all from Richard.

Where are you? I need my tablet. I have court!

Mickey, if you're not here in ten minutes I'm going to lose my case!

Damn it, Michaela, call me right now!

I actually started to laugh, remembering where his tablet ended up. Whoops. And for the first time ever I felt zero remorse. I texted him the dumpster's location and deleted then blocked his number before checking the next message.

I was expecting backlash from Judy. My boss's text was all caps.

MICHAELA. MY OFFICE! NOW! Which meant, naturally, I was hours late answering.

CHAPTER TWENTY SEVEN

After a moment of debate that made my insides cringe with regret and anxiety, I decided to take the coward's route and let Judy have the night to cool off before I spoke to her. I'd go to her office first thing and explain everything, beg her forgiveness. We'd been working together long enough, surely she'd understand? I'd tell her about Paul, get my life straightened out.

Somehow, I managed to convince myself and ignored the lingering hits of nervous tension that lingered and woke from moment to moment, reminding me of looming dread I had to deal with in the morning.

Meanwhile, I thought about Jones as I

watered my cactus, wondering where she was and then, because of Elliot, thought about my father. The idea of having him in my life after all this time was as foreign as doing what the handsome photographer had done, dumping his life and starting fresh. But I liked the idea. So, with tea poured, I sat down at my computer and opened my blog to a new post.

What did I want?

I shouldn't have been surprised the answers didn't leap piecemeal from my hands and tell me exactly what to do from here. If anything, despite knowing I wanted to write, I couldn't even type those words. Instead, I caught myself rotating slowly back and forth in my office chair before finally sighing and closing the laptop lid to retreat to bed, suddenly exhausted.

My waking thought the next morning was sheer panic as the truth of yesterday bowled me over and kicked my ass. What was I thinking? Yesterday was a blur, like I'd gone into some kind of trance that made me a madwoman. Yes, that was it. I had lost my mind. I was going to have to check in to the hospital or something, accept the straight jacket they made me wear and three pills a day.

I was going to lose my job. I couldn't lose my job. How would I survive?

I rushed to work, knowing I had to look like

a lunatic bursting into Judy's office before 8AM. Unsurprised to find her already there.

"Get in here." Judy always came across as a strong, no-nonsense woman I never wanted to cross. I'd spent all these years on her good side. Wow, had that changed. With her round cheeks flushed dark red and eyes narrowed under that solid fringe of bangs she wore like a suit of armor, I'd never seen her look so angry. "Can you please explain why Mr. Pekette is suing our firm and blames it on you?" She lurched to her feet, visibly furious while my heart and mind battled it out with the looming sense of finality of this conversation. "And where you were all day yesterday? Have you lost your mind?"

I opened my mouth to try to respond only to have her shake her index finger at me.

"You are not to talk. Do you understand? You will apologize to Mr. Pekette and you will beg him to forgive you. And you will get him to drop his lawsuit threat, my girl." But, it wasn't my fault his project was over budget. "Or Michaela, I swear, I'm firing your ass right here and now."

I was getting sick and tired of my own tears, but I couldn't help them. "Yes, ma'am."

"Get the hell out of my office."

I left, closing the door behind me, heading toward my desk and the seat I'd sat at for the past twenty years. It felt like an extension of myself. My eyes were clouded with moisture so I didn't realize Paul was right in front of me until I was too late to stop him from grabbing my shoulders, trying to pull me in for a hug.

"Not good, Mick. You okay?" His touch felt poisonous, acidic. Suddenly he was trying to kiss my neck, touch me in places he had no right to touch me. I pushed him away while I looked up to see Lauren's disdainful glare and lost my mind all over again.

"Get away from me!" I knew I was shouting, voice cracking and warbling, but I couldn't stop myself. "And don't touch me ever again." He toppled as I shoved against him, looking around as the few staff in the office at this hour watched, his face flushed, turning dark red.

"Whatever," he hissed then, leaning in with spiteful vitriol written all over his face. "I hope you get fired, you slut."

I stared, shaking and cold as he went back to his own cubicle and pretended nothing happened. For my part? I spun and headed for the women's bathroom and the chance to cry it out.

I was shocked when Lauren followed me inside and flipped the lock on the main door, trapping us inside. She turned toward me with enough disdain on her face I cringed, just wanting her to leave me alone. My day—my life—was going badly enough, thanks.

"You're pathetic." She'd never said anything

like that to me before, preferring her cold arrogance to direct verbal attacks. Honestly, it was worst then a physical blow.

I scrambled for more excuses, my favorite. "I didn't know what I was doing when Paul—" I hated that I felt like I needed to explain anything to her.

"This isn't about Paul." Lauren cut through the air with one hand like she was chopping down the giant tree of mistakes I'd made with one blow. "He's slime and associating with him is just bad judgment. But that's your business outside of work." She shook her head, crossing her arms over her chest to glare at me. "You crying all the time, whining about your life? That's what makes you so pathetic. You're weak." She tossed that golden hair of hers like doing so meant she was better than me. "Get a backbone." She turned to go, snapping the lock open. "I'm tired of cleaning up your messes. I want the best for this firm and you're the weak link. I'm glad you're going to get fired." And then she deliberately walked away.

I knew she was right, had zero argument. I was pathetic. And I couldn't lose this job.

I returned to my desk, dazed, stunned, before putting my head down and getting back to the job. Punctuated part way through my day by a short and painful moment in Judy's office when I had to mumble an apology to Mr. Pekette, practically groveling for his forgiveness. It was a vague and amorphous moment I barely remembered later, likely because I refused to acknowledge just how far I'd fallen. All I did recall when it was over was Mr. Pakette and Judy openly blaming me for the overage on his project, something that clearly had nothing to do with me, but gave both my boss and the client the ability to smooth things over.

"I fully expect this firm to step up and complete the job as contracted." Mr. Pekette glared at me. "If this isn't resolved to my satisfaction, we will have a problem."

Judy quickly agreed before ushering him out. When she turned to me, her grim expression made me want to crumble. "I have no idea how this project got so bungled, Mickey, but your name is on it." I fish lipped, wanting to protest. No, this wasn't mine, I never led projects, she knew that. "I thought I could trust you, but apparently not." Wait, what was happening? "Get back to work and find a way to cover the overages it's going to cost to make this right. This is one major fuckup and from someone I didn't expect, you of all people."

I stumbled back to my desk, unable to believe my life had spiraled into this. I passed Paul as he snubbed me and, at least, was grateful for that. One thing was certain, I was done with him for good.

A review of the file showed my signature on many documents, signing off on plans I had never even seen. What the hell happened? This slowly building dread rose up from the pit of my stomach while I clenched against it. Who was trying to get me fired? I needed to start looking for a solution, but paused a moment.

Was it worth it? Hands shaking, knowing I had no choice, I dialed a familiar number, just wanting her voice at the other end of the line. Needing it.

"Sorry you missed me, but, hey! Don't fret, pumpkin. Leave me a message and I'll call you back. Unless you're Tommy. Dude, you're a dick. Have a great day!"

Even telling off a guy in her phone message, Jones sounded as happy and full of life as always. Why was that so depressing? Oh, right. Because I wasn't.

Without further delay I got back to work, pulling strings, calling in favors. Turned out the project wasn't as overspent as Mr. Pekette had claimed and that despite his utter loss of composure, we were only about $20,000 out. I had enough connections with contractors and suppliers that I was able to fix the overage in a few hours and, upon delivering the updated file to Judy, called the client personally in her presence.

To my relief, his response was eager and excited. "Thank you for correcting your mistakes so quickly, Miss O'Keefe," he said over speakerphone while Judy's stern unhappiness relaxed. "I take it this will be the last we hear of it?"

I was hoping she might see this as a good sign, but I got nothing from Judy as I left her office and, spent but at least out of the fire, made a hasty retreat.

Jones still hadn't called back and, for the first time, I started to worry. Yes, she was unavailable at times, off living her own life, but she never left me hanging this long. Loneliness was far more common than I was willing to admit and, to my surprise, I subconsciously ended up in front of my Mother's door.

What was I doing here? I almost left, but my traitor hand rose, buzzed to be let in. She answered, sounding happy.

"Who is it?"

"Mickey, Mom." I knew I sounded hesitant. I hadn't exactly left on good terms.

"Oh, dear." Yup, there went her happiness. "I wasn't expecting you." I was about to turn and leave when the buzzer sounded. "Come up."

And, though I knew it was a terrible idea but with nowhere else to go, I willingly entered the lion's den.

CHAPTER TWENTY EIGHT

Mom was waiting at the open door to her apartment, her equally open arms wide toward me, waiting for an embrace. That knocked me off a little, the desperate need for her attention exactly what I'd come here for. I stepped in for a hug and instantly started to cry, hating that I thought of Lauren when I did.

I wasn't expecting such affection from Mom. "What's this, dear?" She hugged me tight. "You're going to get bags under your eyes." She pushed me back, frowning, touching my cheek with her fingertips, carefully manicured nails scraping over my skin. "Crying looks good on some people, but not you, Michaela. Your complexion can't handle it." She tsked at me before leading me inside and closing the door, guiding me to her living room. "Now just tell me what's going on, without the drama."

I swallowed tears and nodded, trying a little smile. Because if Mom was making an effort, maybe there was hope for us. Did she feel badly for how she treated me? For putting Richard first? I collapsed on her white leather couch. "Mom, how could they? Did you know they were trying, after all those years I wanted children? Then he gets pregnant with the woman he cheats on with me? I can't handle it." Mom cleared her throat, looking uncomfortable, but I forged on, needing her to hear everything, for once. "I ended up yelling at a client yesterday and almost got fired over it. I feel like I'm drowning and I don't know how to save myself."

If I'd been expecting her sympathy, I'd been sorely mistaken. "Oh Michaela." She waved one hand in front of her face as if some foul odor had entered her domain. "Always with the dramatics. Please. Everyone has had a hard life. You're nothing special."

She might as well have slapped me. But Mom wasn't done. Mom was never done.

"Yes, you're right. Richard is a vile snake, cheating on you. I will never forgive him for that. He brought shame to our family. If you could have just kept him happy, he wouldn't have strayed, though, would he?" I sat there and took the punishment I'd obviously come here to obtain, getting colder and smaller and more weary by the moment as my mother rattled on. "I've tried my whole life to teach you girls it's vital for your survival to have your man eat out of the palm of your hand." She waved that manicure at me. "If he's not, if he's even a little indifferent to you? Well, you can forget it." She sighed in defeat, like this was all my fault. "You never did have the strength it took to keep a man like him, and now you're complaining your life is falling apart? Take some responsibility for a change and stop whining." She crossed her arms over her chest and, looking like Lauren's posture of disdain, finished me off. "I'm so tired of listening to it."

I couldn't say a word, too stupefied. Was she right? Was I the reason Richard cheated on me? Who I was hung in the balance and I didn't know who to turn to for help because the woman in front of me wasn't doing me any favors. Or was she? Elliot seemed to think I needed more selfishness, to not listen to anyone else but myself. But what if who I was didn't believe in me, either?

Tara showed up before I could sort my thoughts, her sing song voice repulsive to me. "Mom, I got the flowers you like." As soon as she spotted me her nose tilted higher, tight smile fading. "Oh, hello, Mickey." Just like that, she vanished into the kitchen.

I was about to rise, to leave, now certain I'd made a huge mistake coming here, when Mom called out to my sister. "Tara, come in here. We need your advice." No, we didn't. Tara was the last person in the world I wanted to empty my heart out to. Not the sister who always judged me and never supported me, not even when my marriage unraveled. But before I could just run away, Tara reappeared, faint frown barely hidden by the injections she'd been getting the last year or so.

"Yes, Mom?" She didn't even look at me. What did I do to her, exactly?

"Do you think Richard left Michaela for no reason?" Wow, Mom, how tactful and kind of you.

Tara's nose wrinkled, the button end adorable if she wasn't looking at me suddenly like I was a burden on both of them. "What's this? Richard again? Seriously, Mickey." I cringed and retreated inwardly, looking down at my hands clenched in my lap. "You need to get over this." Tara exhaled in a puff of impatience. "He's moved on. He's the happiest I've ever seen him." Because he was never happy with me. "It's always about you and your cheesy production, making us all uncomfortable, like Sunday night. You're a train wreck, sister." She sniffed then. "Your

Broadway musical isn't worth the price of admission." And, with that, my flesh and blood turned again to busy herself in the kitchen as if she hadn't just torn me apart, humming loudly enough it was impossible to miss how happy she sounded.

Leaving was a blur of Mom hugging me again, seemingly pleased with the conversation until I was out in the cold, chilled by more than the October temperature. I was almost home, just about to open the door to my refuge, when I heard the elevator ding down the hall. My mind registered they'd fixed it, an odd and disjointed thought, right before a storm blew through and barreled right toward me.

"Michaela!" I'd never seen Richard angry. Bored, irritated, stern, indifferent. But never angry. Until now, that was. Maybe I should have been concerned by his rage, or afraid. Instead, weary and at the limit of my own endurance, I could barely muster interest. Besides, he really looked like a cartoon character with his eyes bulging and his cheeks all red like that. "Where have you been?" He didn't stop in his demanding diatribe long enough for me to answer, not like I had the energy to muster anything anyway. "I needed my notes yesterday. I trusted you with this, and you let me down. Why aren't you picking up your phone, or answering my messages?"

He looked me up and down like he didn't know me. Well, he didn't, no more than I knew him, apparently. "Where the hell is my tablet? Give it to me."

I looked down at his extended hand, register his snapping fingers as he commanded me to relinquish his property. I couldn't look him in the face, remembering the feeling of triumph I felt when I defied him. "I lost it." I said.

"Excuse me?" Richard's volume climbed, loud enough Mrs. Barrow peeked out her door, scowled, and slammed it again. "How could you lose it? Where were you? Tell me what happened."

His questions shot at me like bullets I didn't have the capacity to dodge. Caught between his raging body and my unlocked door, I finally felt fear twinge as he loomed, hands now fisted at his sides. I'd never worried Richard might strike me. He'd never been that passionate. But now? I had to admit it felt like a distinct possibility.

"I... I dropped it." Wait, hadn't I texted him the image of the dumpster? And I was a terrible liar. He had to have known I wasn't being straight with him.

Richard's rage just increased. "*Dropped* it? *Where* Michaela? I *need* it." I could smell his breath, the coffee and something with onions he'd consumed, see the vein in the center of his forehead pulse, feel the pressure of the heat of his body as he closed the distance between us further. Gone was any longing for us to be together again, replaced by the sick feeling in my gut I'd never known the man I'd shared so many years of my life with. "It's not only for this case." He swallowed hard, wiping at his damp upper lip with one hand, fisting it again next to my shoulder as it fell while I choked on fear. "I could be charged if someone gets some of the files that are on its hard drive. Where did you drop it?"

I drew a deep breath, knowing the fastest way to get rid of him was to come clean. "I threw it in the dumpster at a job site."

Richard's face went slack. Utterly and completely slack, like whoever inhabited his body vanished for a second, went off somewhere to check on something they'd forgotten and left his husk of a shell to fend for itself. The absolute worst response I could have had to that expression? Laughter.

Guess what bubbled up?

I bit down on my lip to stop myself from exploding from the need, but I know he saw it. He had to have seen it. There was no repressing it and, though I'm sure it was triggered by fear and tension and my horrible, horrible day boiling down to either giggling my head off or collapsing in a teary heap, Richard couldn't have known that.

And then the alien presence that was Richard's operation system burst back into life like a switch being thrown. "You Did WHAT? HOW? WHY? WHERE?" His big arms rose, hands grasping my upper arms. Richard pushed me forcefully into my door, my back thudding hard enough I oofed out my breath, not hurt but definitely shaken. "You don't care about anyone but yourself, do you?" He let me go, but the threat of his presence didn't leave. If anything, the fear of him returned, rose in a wave ready to crash over me. Where was Mrs. Barrow now? Was she calling the cops? My hand scrambled behind me, hunting for the knob to my door, desperate to escape him while he ranted in a low, trembling voice, his mouth so close to mine I could have kissed him if he didn't look like he was ready to murder me and hide my body. "I can't believe I put up with you for all those years." The part of me that remained rational, tiny as it was, understood he was purposely trying to hurt me. And it worked. "I couldn't wait to get away from you." He spit that in my face. "You want to know why we didn't have kids, Mick?" I didn't. I really didn't. Not now, not like this. "I was terrified they would end up like you."

The physical assault was bad enough, but I could deal. This? I couldn't handle this. I couldn't help it, though I despised myself my weakness, Lauren's disdain flashing in my head all over again as I started to cry.

I think Richard took my breakdown as some kind of triumph. He relented, at least, pushing off from me like he was satisfied he'd destroyed me utterly. "That tablet better still be there when I look for it, Michaela, or I'll be back." He held very still, fury just under the surface. "You're not going to like it if I come back." With that, he spun and strode off the way he'd come.

CHAPTER TWENTY NINE

A half hour later, I'd practically dug a trench in my laminate floor with all my pacing. Richard hadn't returned, so I could only hope he wouldn't and since the police hadn't showed up I could only assume my neighbor had decided I wasn't worth the effort.

I'd talked myself out of the fear he'd actually turn violent, though. Not Richard. Still, as I circled my apartment trying to settle and completely incapable of it, my mind raced in search of something I could do just in case. Who could I call? No one I could think of would consider getting involved in my mess. Yes, I did linger a moment on Elliot. He'd been there for me with Paul, but that had been a wrong place, wrong time arrangement. Besides, no way was I dragging him into this.

A text flashed, pulling me out of my nervous anxiety to leap on my phone. Jones, thank god.

Except, she didn't pick up when I called and when I finally checked her message I felt the crush of disappointment she, too, had let me down.

Sorry, I'll make it up to you. Have some shit to clean up. You are AMAZING and Richard can suck ass.

The elevator dinged in the hall outside and I jumped when a door slams. This was ridiculous. I couldn't stay here, waiting for Richard to maybe come back and do something to me despite arguing with myself he just wasn't that kind of person. Because honestly, I wasn't so sure anymore.

I grabbed my coat and slunk from my building, heading down the street, stopping myself outside the now familiar bar before shaking my head and turning back. Even as Elliot flashed in my head one more time.

He said call him anytime. If I needed him. And he'd always been kind. More than ever I needed a shoulder to lean on.

The young man behind the desk at Elliot's hotel smiled at me so I couldn't have looked too desperate. "Can I help you?"

"I'm trying to reach one of your guests." I gulped as I realized what I was doing, calling on him like this at his hotel, that it wouldn't look good, would it? But that didn't stop me. "Elliot Parker?"

"One moment." He picked up the phone, dialed a number. "Yes, sir. There's a woman here to see you." He raised his eyebrows at me in question and I tried a smile that trembled only a little.

"It's Mickey."

He repeated my name into the handset before nodding and hanging up. "Room 355, ma'am." He pointed then toward the back hall. "Elevators right over there."

Nervous, I nodded thanks and headed for the doors, waiting a moment for the elevator to arrive, still debating leaving until they whooshed open in welcome. I picked at a loose thread on my jacket, knowing this was a terrible idea. I needed to go home, face the music if Richard did return. But before I knew it my traitorous feet were in front of Elliot's door.

I knocked with my heart in my throat, hearing his voice call out. "Just a minute." And then his door opened and I was staring into his bare chest, jeans hugging his hips low without support of a belt, feet bare.

He knew I was coming, had enough time to at least wear that much, I guess, hair tousled, eyes sleepy. Had I woken him? I should have felt badly. Instead, my insides growled. How could he look so comfortable and yummy when my life was falling apart?

Elliot stepped aside, and I made my way into his room without a word, turning at the last second. He met me halfway and then I was in his arms, pulling his head down to my level. I forced my mouth onto his, trying desperately to open his with my tongue, wanting him, wanting something I couldn't define or describe.

Elliot gently grasped my upper arms where Richard's hands had left small bruises and slowly but firmly pushed me back until he was standing at arm's length. I cringed, flinched, waited for his anger. Instead, his green and gold eyes looked so sad I wanted to cry all over again.

"Are you okay, Mickey?" There was more concern in his eyes than I could bear, more than I was worthy of.

Instead of asking for help, I lashed out, shocked at my reaction to his kindness when this was what I'd come for, his support and help. "Don't you want to sleep with me? What's wrong with you? Aren't you a man?"

To my shock, as I broke down and sobbed, he didn't show any signs of offense. Quite the opposite.

"What happened?" He continued to hold

me away from him, big hands gentle but reminding me too much of Richard.

I choked on the sobs and forced myself still, bitterness rising. "Nothing. I just wanted to see you." I could hear how foolish and fake that sounded, made worse when my mouth wouldn't stop. "Fuck you." So coarse, not like me at all. Where did that come from?

Elliot's reaction only added to my frustration, not a hint of anything in it for me to fight against. "Not like this, Mickey." I could have argued with him, but he still sounded sad. Not disappointed, just hurting, as if he wanted to help me but knew better. So did I, not that knowledge was helping when my heart needed more. "You know I like you." I guess so. "But this is a terrible idea." He escorted me toward the door while I tried to prevent it, scanning the room, spotting photos on his bed. He must have been proofing and fallen asleep.

Desperate to stop my exit, to make a connection, I tried appealing to his art. "Can I see your work?"

Turned out that was the wrong way to go. For the first time he sounded stern rather than kind. "You need to leave."

Couldn't he see I needed him? No, not him specifically, and maybe that was the problem and we both knew it. I was seeking, yes. Anything that would make me feel alive. Which wasn't fair to him, or to me.

"I just need someone I can trust to be with right now." I sagged in his grasp, willing to admit that much, at least.

He finally relented, pausing at the door, hands no longer holding me away from him, now gently stroking my arms. "I do care about you, more then I was expecting to. But I can't sleep with you, not like this." He was right and I nodded, swallowed, ashamed of myself but surprised when he groaned softly, face clearly conflicted. "God, I want to. But I want you empowered first." Maybe I shouldn't have taken that as a positive, considering he was telling me I was weak and useless now, but knowing he wanted me actually helped. At least someone did, someone who cared enough to put me first. "I would hate to think I'd taken advantage of you. We'd never get the chance to go somewhere. Does that make sense? Because I'd love that, Mick. Someday. With someone like you."

I barely heard him, to be honest. That slow stroke down my arms, even through my jacket? Fired every cell in my body, building heat where there had only been cold. The barest of pressure or not, as I inhaled to try to reply I felt our energy jump to connect to each other in the same moment his eyes went wide.

I stared up into his hypnotic green gaze, drowning in it, the flecks of gold. I begged him to kiss me with my eyes, half opening my lips as his touch moved ever so slowly up and down my arms in that same motion that was meant, I think, to soothe me but had become so much more. Who knew such a simple caress could create such a fire?

We didn't speak. We didn't need to. Chemistry did all the talking for us. Elliot held fast, not losing his control but no longer trying to usher me out. Instead, he seemed willing to give me what I craved, if still on his terms. Did he know how the electricity his touch generated flowed everywhere through me, nerve endings jumping from the back of my neck to my toes, most of it descending to center between my legs? I spread them without thought, craving his touch, this time without the desperation I'd felt when I'd arrived, the intensity stronger, if anything, fed by real connection.

Still Elliot held true, though he surprised me as he leaned forward, lightly kissing my mouth. I couldn't help the groan that escaped, pushing my lips closer to his, as one of his hands found the small of my back. The ghost of his touch through layers of fabric teased me, making me squirm. His own soft exhalation vibrated with the faintest sound as his head dipped, delicious tongue tasting my neck.

I lost it completely, body convulsing without my permission, his tongue digging deeper into my flesh. The assault brought a greater wave of reaction and, with a cry that I couldn't control and a spasm of contraction that surprised me with its intensity and sudden crest, I orgasmed on the spot.

Elliot supported me as I flexed my fingers deep into the muscles of his bare back, knees weak from the sensations washing over me. He held me tight while lightly kissing my forehead, lips brushing lovingly over my skin. I felt safe there with him as the orgasm faded and left me shaking and breathless. The safest I'd felt in a long while. I looked up at him and smiled, speaking before I could stop myself.

"Thank you." Did I really just thank him for... wow. And yet, I couldn't help but feel completely open, trusting him utterly. Naïve, maybe, but he'd only ever been kind.

He hugged me then, almost as intense a sensation as the orgasm itself, if only because I hadn't been held in so long it was a foreign and shockingly intimate sensation. I could hear his heartbeat as I rested my cheek against his wide chest, loving the feeling. We stayed that way for a long time, neither one of us wanting to let go. At least, he made no effort to do so and I happily clung to him and let his warmth fill me up.

I could have this. I knew it, breathed it in, accepted it. But I had to find myself first, didn't I? That's what Elliot said. And he was right. This was amazing, awesome, beautiful.

But the woman I was now? She'd find a way to ruin it. And I never wanted to ruin what I discovered I wanted so very much, with Elliot or another man like him.

A man just like him.

I finally spoke, barely a whisper, wishing I could change everything and knowing I had to. "I know your leaving, and I have a lot to figure out on my own." He nodded into my hair. "But, Elliot, you've shown me I can do it, too. What you did. I want what you have." He tightened his grip on me a moment before easing up again. "If something does happen between us, I want to know I'm whole and can bring all of me to you." I smiled up at him, realizing how exposed he was. How willing to give me anything.

He lightly kissed my lips. "I look forward to that, beautiful lady."

We parted, the door closing behind me and when I stood alone outside his room, with the magnetism of him lingering on me, I hugged myself as though my arms were his.

I needed to figure out how to make myself happy. To feel safe, satisfied, loved. I deserved it, wanted it more than anything. Had to find it on my own.

But how?

CHAPTER THIRTY

By the time I reached my front door, "I know I want this" and "How can I do this?" bouncing back and forth were giving me a headache. It was easier to just do what I'd always done. Better to know the heartbreak pending instead of something new ready to crush my spirit. And yet, I knew there had to be a better way.

As a distraction, I opened my emails, a guiding light shining in a message from Jones.

Mick, I love this character. I want to see what happens next. Gabby is awesome. Strong, sensual and open. Love love love her. Keep going. XOXOX

And there, attached to the bottom of the

message, was the chapter I originally deleted. My curiosity, fired from Elliot's touch, fueled me to open the doc and start reading it again. But this time from an open and playful perspective.

On finishing my first and only completed chapter, I had to admit I loved it. Really and truly loved it. Yes, there was work to do, naturally. Of course I had edits and tweaks and some fleshing out to do, no pun intended. But I was finally willing to admit I wasn't the failure I'd let myself believe.

I could do this.

My body physically relaxed as I settled into that truth. Time to give Gabriella a voice and, in doing so, free mine at the same time.

The next several hours I spent in the zone, not thinking, just writing. I'd been in this place before, but not at this level, the euphoric feeling cresting and rising and cresting again almost like the orgasms I wrote about.

Every once and a while my thoughts derailed for a moment, judging my work, trying to force me off the tracks. But the joy of the writing overrode all previous behavior as I flexed my creativity, choosing at last to just see what might happen if I didn't stop.

By the time I finished, drained but happy, hugging myself, proud of what I'd done, I glanced up at the clock on the wall. How was it 5AM? I'd been writing nonstop for six hours? I couldn't stop the laugh out loud, the amazed daze of delight. Now, how to keep this momentum going? This feeling of freedom that fed my soul?

I inhaled before giving a quick skim of what I'd written, almost afraid to allow myself that retrospective. Instead of my usual criticism, though, I realized very quickly the characters I wrote about felt very close to, if not exactly like, the people in my own life.

Panic hit me. I couldn't use any of this, could I? They'd know and instantly hate me. Except a soft thought interrupted, one I didn't want to connect to, whispered the truth. This was my baby, the child I'd been left with. No Richard to control it, no one to tell me I wasn't ready or couldn't follow through. I sighed deeply with understanding. Maybe this was the motherhood I'd been meant to fulfill?

I saved the document instead of deleting it, my first instinct. That small voice kept whispering I couldn't just throw away what I'd made. It was precious, deserved to live. Like I did. Decision made, I tenderly closed the lid of my computer, placing my hand on the top, sending loving thoughts into it. A funny gesture, but one that felt true to me.

How could expending so much energy make me feel so renewed? I caught myself humming while getting really to go to work.

I actually loved my life. Imagine that.

There was a buzz in my mind, like a kind of high, one I enjoyed immensely. I even caught myself smiling outwardly. The simple act of walking into the office was done with a floating, breezy sensation I'd never experienced before. Everything seemed different to me, more colorful, almost sparkly, as if some gray cloud had been lifted from my vision. I noticed the cubicle dividers for the first time, flimsy, cheap place board, held together with tiny hooks. The paint on the walls? All cream and gray. How uncreative. My sense of smell even seemed heightened, burned coffee scent assaulting my nostrils. The carpet under my pumps seemed the only splash of color, but even that was trying too hard, swirls of greens, golds and blues clashing in overdone waves of fiber.

How weird not to have noticed before just how tired this whole place felt. And despite my lack of sleep, my emotional day previous, I myself didn't feel that weariness the space seemed to suffer from, though the temptation of coffee lured me toward the staff room.

I made a fresh pot after dumping the mess someone else made, singing a wordless song as I waited for the perking to end. The pot was heavy when I finally lifted it free, aiming the lip at the top of my mug.

"Don't take it all." I glanced at Paul who lunged for the pot. "I just made it and everyone always takes it before I get any." I didn't bother telling him I dumped his wretched attempt down the sink, letting him take the pot from me. Gone was my discomfort with his presence, that feeling of intimidation he'd told everyone about our encounter. Instead, I tilted my head as I studied him, seeing him as though for the first time. I was amazed at his small, cold eyes, how they tried to bore into me, his slender frame bubbled in front by the beginning of a soft belly, shoulders rounded in. He was barely taller than me, beginnings of wrinkles around his dark eyes, hair thinning in the front, too. I'd never noticed such details before.

Most striking, though? The fact he seemed like he was hiding from something. I observed his posture with clinical detachment. Why was he hunched like that? Protecting his heart? One thing was certain, he looked nothing like the person I thought I knew. Instead, I realized I'd only ever seen the shell of the man.

Pity welled as I answered with empathy. "We can always make more, Paul."

He huffed at me then stormed off like I'd insulted him. Had I? As I moved toward my desk, I spotted Lauren and, before I could stop myself, smiled at her.

Was this what she was talking about? Taking charge of myself? Hard not to feel the difference now. Damn, I loved it.

It didn't matter to me when Lauren didn't return my expression. If anything, it empowered me more. Because it really didn't matter to me one way or the other. It was so hard to resist the urge to laugh out loud as I sat to begin my work for the day.

"Michaela, can you grab the art pieces for the Whenchel project? They're archived downstairs." Judy barely looked at me before turning back to her office. She seemed to have gone back to her normal treatment of me, so that was a good sign, right?

Feeling great and not in the slightest snubbed, I smiled with a cheerful, "Yes, ma'am." and grabbed the key by the door to unlock the storage room in the basement. I couldn't stop thinking about my book while I waited for the elevator. Was it written all over me as the doors opened to the most pleasant surprise and those delicious green eyes? My face felt like it was about to break in half as I beamed in response to Elliot's appearance and I lunged for him, taking his hand as my mouth took off.

"Oh my god, I have to talk to you." His own smile infectious, he held the door open for me to enter, both of us ignoring the fact he'd meant to get off.

"Do tell." Green eyes tease me, the lift of a smile on his full lips. I stood so very close, still holding his hand, feeling his heat next to me.

My body memory was fresh enough I flushed all over recalling our last meeting, but I was so excited by what happened after that I gushed on.

"After I left you" I said, smiling shyly up at him as I hesitated one moment in acknowledgement of what happened, "I went home and read this story I started last week." He nodded for me to go one while I hopped on my toes in excitement. "I wasn't sure if it was any good, you know? But, Elliot! It is and I'm so excited. I couldn't stop writing. Last night I just kept at it all night." Wasn't lost on me the innuendo tied to our encounter the evening before bled through as if the words I chose had nothing to do with my book. "I didn't even sleep. It was like magic."

Elliot's growing grin peaked in a laugh as he tugged me to him and hugged me. Because he was, after all, the perfect person to confess this to.

"I think I know what you're talking about." He exhaled into my ear before letting me go, my excited vibration zinging between us. "That thing that sparks you and fills you up, right?" He didn't stop his touch, reaching out to feather across my hand as I went on.

Except my recollection of what that touch could do to me was so close to the surface a groan escaped my lips at contact. I expected him to pull away. Instead, his eyes twinkled with mischief, just as the doors opened on the empty crypt this building used as storage.

I led him inside, wavering between the passion I felt for him and the equal fire burning inside me for the book I wanted to go home and write.

"I would love to read it, Mickey." His deep voice sounded sincere, happy. "That's magnificent." Hard to miss the hint of heat he let escape in those two words. His hand cupped my neck, face moving in closer, looking down into me, honestly into the depths of me, my soul. His other hand ran the length of my arm and finally reached my hand, fingers twining with mine. I'd never experienced this kind of connection before and found it instantly intoxicating.

"You inspired me." He had. The sexual tension between us, his support and kindness? Exactly what I'd needed in a lifetime of hurt, disappointment, judgement. "I couldn't stop. It was like I was someone else." I giggled into my free hand, the other still trapped by his. "Elliot, I *love* it."

He kissed me deeply without warning, his own moan escaping his mouth at the same time it engulfed mine. My need for him surged back to the forefront, but without the desperate need I'd felt before. Instead, we enjoyed each other, the mutual contact, my nipples hardening under his gentle touch as he stroked them through the fabric of my blouse and bra. Such pleasure and pain at the same time, I leaned into him until he increased the pressure.

The desire to feel his flesh against mine smothered everything else, including propriety, my craving to taste last night all over again taking me over. I pushed my chest into him, rubbing my body against his. I could feel the bulge between us react to me through the pressure. We groaned in unison. He moved his mouth to my neck and, remembering last night, I breathed deep, arching my back in anticipation of the rush to come.

There was only him, then, guiding me deeper into the storage space, pressing me against the wall, tucked away from the watchful eyes of the security cameras, the closed elevator doors. He artfully kneaded the muscles in my neck with his tongue, tracing my collar bone before returning to my mouth, his eager and hungry lips driving me crazy. I felt a release between my legs, my body more than ready and willing than even last night's encounter.

"What's the meaning of this?" Paul's appearance put an instant end to our intimacy, my regret deep and sharp while I tugged at my clothes, Elliot's shame clear on his face. "This is our workplace, Michaela. Way to be totally unprofessional." Like he should talk. Before I could say as much, he turned to reenter the elevator door we didn't hear open. Elliot immediately turned to me regret sharp enough I knew we were done. At least, for now. Forever?

"I am so sorry, Mickey." His flushed cheeks and worried expression made me sigh. Why wasn't I more freaked about it? I just couldn't muster concern. "This wasn't my intent. And at your work. Seriously, I'm so sorry. I hope I don't get you in trouble."

I shrugged, laughed. "Damn, he couldn't wait like two more minutes?"

Elliot grinned, then laughed. "Needed longer than two minutes," he said. Winked.

I winked back. "I guess I should get these pieces to Judy." More regret, but this time for the opportunity lost.

"Would you like some help?" Did he know howl adorable and vulnerable and yummy he was right at that moment?

"I'll be fine," I said. "Best for the two of us to part ways, maybe? Just in case Paul said something to Judy."

Elliot stopped me, one hand catching mine. "If you're up for continuing what we started, I'll be at the hotel."

This was a change from yesterday. Had I shifted so very far, so fast? Yes, yes, I had. Even I knew it.

Like I had any plans to turn down his offer.

"I'll see you later."

Our hands parted and we did, too. It took me a few minutes to get myself calmed down, the pounding of my heartbeat, the tingling in my skin and I was still grinning when I hunt down Judy's request.

The old me tried to reassert herself. I was going to get my heart broken. He was leaving soon. What was I thinking? Oh, I knew exactly what I was thinking. And all of my thoughts were naughty.

Still spinning from our encounter, I lugged my prize back to the office, knowing I had to focus, but pretty sure my day was shot.

This is what men do to you, they throw you off your game. Mom, lingering.

At least I wasn't bitter, I shot back at her imaginary disappointment. And now, I knew, I never would be.

Judy's commanding voice echoed my name the moment I stepped off the elevator and, still holding the ugly sculpture she'd sent me for, I spun toward her door and froze. Paul, his face contorted with malice, walked away from my boss who jabbed her finger in my direction.

"Michaela." She crossed her arms over her chest. "In here. Now!"

All of my newfound sparkle died. Judy's anger terrified me. I think I already knew how this was going to end, and tried to talk as I closed the door. But she was in a froth, tossing her hands and her mind made up, silencing me before I could speak in my defense.

"I have no idea what's happened to you the last few days," she snarled, "but I'm done. I'd been planning on letting you go anyway, to be honest." She blew out a sharp exhale while my whole world crumbled around me. Just when I'd really made a change, this had to happen. Why now? "We're downsizing, and you're the weak link. But damn it, Mickey, I was hoping to save your job, at least for a few more months. But now? Sex in the storage room?" She turned her computer around, showing me the beginning of my embrace with Elliot. "I just can't protect you now."

I stared at the image unfolding, knew there was nothing I could say. While Judy said the rest.

"You're fired." She turned her back on me. "Get out."

CHAPTER THIRTY ONE

I sat, numb and slightly confused, on my train home, looking down at the tiny box on my lap. There wasn't much in there, for all. A small daisy bobble plant Jones gave me, some gum I dug out of the back of my top drawer and a handful of pictures. Mostly of places I wanted to visit.

I guess I had time now, if no income to pay for it. Was that hysteria threatening to make me giggle over the thought? What happened? How did I let this happen? As I played back my forced kindness, always conforming, never making waves until the last few days, I realized that was the problem, right? Of course I was the disposable one. I never showed initiative.

What was I going to do now? I could feel myself slipping back into my old self like some kind of wall slamming up to protect me. One after another, until I was surrounded by darkness and grief and despair.

It wasn't until I was actually inside my apartment I registered something was wrong, I was so lost in my own confusion and fear. But the war zone that had been orderly and clean just an hour before finally jerked me out of my head and into reality.

It was pretty apparent someone had been here and decided to help themselves to my stuff, leaving a mess in their wake. The story of my life. I looked around at the ransacked disaster, crumbling inside while I observed on the detached cusp of collapse. Cupboard doors stood open with dishes smashed on the floor, papers, and books strewn everywhere. My couch had been ripped apart, cushions shredded. What, had they thought I had money tucked away inside them or something?

I held still, perfectly still, positive if I made a single step, drew too deep a breath, I'd fly apart and shatter completely, falling into the same disarray as my apartment. I didn't want to go into my bedroom, staring at the empty place where my TV used to be.

I was going to break. I was positive of it. Until I spotted him, on the floor, and everything shifted. My Little Prick lay squished beyond recognition, soil scattered in a line like a blood spill, his pot shattered. I stared at him, unable to think, feel, move.

And then, like a dam bursting, the walls around me fell outward, the crushing fear and hurt dissipating while I forced a deep inhale, another, before embracing the new resilience I'd managed to muster while I gently saluted the dead cactus.

Stuff. Just stuff. And my laptop was safe in my bag. That was all I cared about right now. The rest? The thieves could have it.

I called 9-1-1. A woman's voice answered almost immediately. "What's your emergency?" I was surprised by how calm I felt, that my voice didn't shake. I quickly told her what happened while she logged my information and sent officers to my place. I exited the apartment on her orders, standing in the hallway with the door wide open, not caring what else had been taken, what things of mine had been violated. It all felt like the past to me, like a purge had begun.

The police officers were nice enough, and pretty thorough. It took about an hour for the handsome young black cop and his older white female counterpart to finish questioning me and looking for evidence.

"Do you know anyone that would want to hurt you?" The woman's brown eyes watched me carefully while I thought about Richard but shook my head. He would have no reason to do this. "Are you living alone?" I nodded this time. "Did you leave your door unlocked?" Had I? But no, I knew better.

It was almost too much, all the questions. My front door stood wide open, exposing me to the neighbors. Mrs. Barrow stared at me with her arms crossed from her own doorway, glaring, though she slammed it in the officer's face when the young man tried to ask her questions. I knew instinctually she blamed me for my own break-in. I was so tired of the haters.

When the cops were finally done, I stared at the new lock on my door my landlord had installed under their watchful eyes. Not like it mattered, did it? If someone wanted to hurt me, they could. They could just break in again, right?

God, why did this feel like a metaphor for my life? And was I going to let anyone break in ever again and cause me pain?

I left the apartment, going to the one place I felt safe. As he opened the door, his first reaction was playful, excited. Until he saw me, really looked. Elliot immediately turned to concern and reached out to bring me close.

Holding him tight, I wanted to feel something other than the horror of my life. I could feel him understand, his body curving against mine, protective, sheltering. As he took my face in his hands, he leaned in slow and deliberate, kissing my mouth. I felt like he was trying to erase everything bad for me through that kiss. I respected his effort and matched his with passion.

I pulled slowly at his shirt, just needing to have his skin against mine. Elliot's body accommodated, the two of us tumbling to the floor. He pulled away from me, hastily unzipping my coat, unbuttoning my shirt. Gentle but insistent, he tugged the fabric free of my waistband and looked down at me, admiration and desire plain on his face.

I loved how he looked at me, like a goddess. I helped him remove my bra, letting my full breasts free. My huge, dark nipples stood out, begging for his touch. His finger lightly trailed down from my face to my neck, following further down across the top of my chest. My body reacted instantly, back arching, seeking his touch to make contact with my most sensitive areas. All the while Elliot watched my every move to make sure I enjoyed it.

Oh, and I enjoyed it.

When his finger finally brushed across one of my nipples, I came. I'd never been one to orgasm so easily, not even with the new, fun toy I'd bought. Elliot seemed able to play my body like a fine violin.

He reacted to my passion, his mouth covering my left breast as his strong arms picked me up, carrying me to his bed. He threw me down, the feeling naughty and thrilling at the same time. I struggled with my skirt, the gorgeous man before me completely naked, shedding his own clothes while standing in front of me, quickly exposed in all his delicious glory. His penis pulsed at me, thick and eager and I stare at it, a mix of longing and faint concern feeding my libido all over again, impossible not to think of Gabby, of Michael.

Richard was no comparison.

Elliot helped with my skirt, my underweartugging them quickly from my body and a thrill exploded at his roughness. My arms rose and I welcomed him to join me. Instead, he spread my legs with his two big hands and plunged his face between them, his mouth on my nether lips. Shocking, exciting, enough I groaned from the surprise, a little uncomfortable at first. I'd never had a man give me oral sex before and I squirmed as I fought my sudden nerves.

Elliot looked up, eyes meeting mine, his dark with passion but face showing his concern. "Is this okay? I can stop."

I shook my head no, forcing myself to relax. Everything he'd done so far had only felt amazing. I needed to trust.

Now with permission, he dove back in and continued his exploration. All tension slid from me easily as his beautiful tongue took over, silencing any rational thought. All I could do was enjoy the new sensations, shuddering with pleasure while he expertly maneuvered his way over the sensitive folds.

Oh. My. God. This was the best-kept secret ever. Yes, I'd heard it was amazing, but I thought that was an exaggeration. Nope, not with the right man doing the job. I could feel his hot breath as his tongue sucked and teased my clitoris. I'd just died and gone to heaven. The muscles in my groin contracted as his tongue entered me. Demanding thoughts took over, hunger for the real thing and I grabbed his face and pulled him up toward me.

Elliot didn't resist when I grasped him, taking firm hold of the pulsing heat of his cock. He leaned in to kiss me but I pulled back a little, shocked at the thought. He'd been somewhere my mind told me wasn't meant for lips.

"You've never tasted yourself before?" I shook my head. "Well, beautiful, you taste like strawberries." He didn't let me stop him then, leaning in to share his tongue with me. At first, I hesitated but surprised myself, kissing him back, tasting sweetness and summer.

My hand flexed around his thick girth, rubbing his tip across my clitoris. I'd never done this before either, but I knew what I wanted, instinct and this feeling of safety in his arms giving me the courage to try. He lifted his head and closed his eyes, the head of his penis slowly entering. God, he was big, but my body didn't let me tense, so ready for him it forced me to relax and let him inside. And suddenly, fearlessly, I wanted to take it all in.

Elliot gave me what I asked for, never denying me, excepting all my offers. Every motion was slow, measured, sending pleasure through my body with each thrust. It was like a dream, his strong arms placed on the small of my back pulling me up toward him with each drive. He leaned down as his length stroked within to devour my other breast. Could I handle all these sensations at once? Overwhelm only fed my pleasure and I panted, strained against him for more. More.

He sped up, his pleasure sounds matching mine, only increasing my passion. Elliot threw his head back, whispering a guttural groan, his girth increasing a moment, the peak of his orgasm releasing inside me. As he came he pushed into me, the deepest I'd ever experienced in my life, the massage of his tip sending another orgasm racing through me into oblivion.

I'd always thought coming together was one of those things every woman wanted. Instead, I was happy to watch him come, see the release cross his face, just before mine took me over. As it relented and let me go, I sagged into his arms, knowing at last what sated felt like.

Elliot slid from me, pulling me toward the hollow of his shoulder, cradling me against his chest. His free hand rose to caress my arm draped naturally across his body, the two of us melded in mutual relaxation.

"I've never had oral sex before." Why was it so hard to admit to him? Because he seemed so knowledgeable, so experienced.

Instead of judgment, as was his way, Elliot just nodded. "And?"

I exhaled against his skin, kissing his shoulder. "It was scary at first. Unnerving?" Another nod from him. "But when I forced myself to relax and went with the flow, it was wonderful. I felt like I went somewhere else, in my body but also I guess my spirit?"

Elliot's lips pressed to my forehead, hugging me gently before reverting to his relaxed state. "Mickey, you deserve all this and more. Pleasure is why we are here." I listened intently. "That's the reason we are here on this earth." Pleasure, huh? Then why was my life so painful? "Society lies to us about how we should live our lives. And we all bought it." He shifted slightly, tilting my head up so I could look in his eyes as he went on. "We aren't here to work till we die, with two weeks of holidays every year and forced retirement at sixty-five." He snorted. "That's the insanity of it. We all believe that's what we deserve!" He was right.

That's what I was raised to believe. "But this, Mick. This is what we deserve." He kissed my forehead, then my nose, finally finding my mouth again.

"But what about work?" I wanted him to keep kissing me, but I had questions. "And money? We need it to survive. Doesn't that mean we have to do what society tells us?"

He laughed, so carefree. "I guess. But wouldn't it be better if you chose something you loved to satisfy those needs? Instead of making someone else happy?" He touched the tip of my nose with one index finger, green eyes serious even though he still wore that delicious smile I loved. It occurred to me I'd failed to tell him about losing my job. Didn't seem important, now. "What would make you happy?"

I answered without hesitation. "Writing. I want to be an author. Not just an author, but a bestselling author." I might as well admit my big dreams, right?

"Okay then, young lady. What do you need to do to make that happen?"

"Well." I paused, feeling a little timid but proud at the same time. "I did write something after, um." I laughed. "After last night." He laughed in return, nodded.

"I'm so proud of you." I couldn't help the glow of delight at his praise. No one had ever been proud of me, had they? Except maybe

Jones. "How did it feel? Don't judge the content." He sounded like he knew what he was talking about. Had he judged himself in the beginning, too? "How did it feel while you were doing it?" He was suddenly intense, focused.

I gave the question the kind of thought it deserved, that he deserved, before answering. "It felt like I was home," I admitted to myself and gasped. My eyes fixed on my hand, lying there on his chest, before I turned my gaze up into his beautiful face. My muse, my lover, the man who gave me the freedom to be. And I smiled so hard I thought my face was going to split in two.

"You just found the secret," he said. "Never listen to anything but what your heart tells you. You are going to be just fine, Michaela. I know it."

All afternoon we matched each other's hunger, enjoying our openness and connection. Never once did he ask me why I was there, how I'd come to join him when I was meant to be at work. Did he know I'd been fired? Maybe. And maybe that was why his message seemed so much more intense to me now.

Late afternoon found us resting in each other's arms, Elliot caressing my skin with lazy hands, just enjoying the moment.

"I am so proud of you, beautiful." His voice

vibrated a bit, emotions on the surface. "You're on your journey and I'm very excited for you." I traced my finger across his chest, playing with his nipple a little as he talked. "You know I'm leaving tomorrow." I hadn't wanted to think about that. "Europe is calling me." I tilted my head to look him in the eye, refusing to let him feel guilt. Not after everything he'd given me. "You have so much you need to explore. I can't, I won't, take that away from you." I would have loved for him to stay. But he was right, as always. I offered him a smile in answer. "If we jumped into a relationship right now, it wouldn't be the kind we both need and deserve." I leaned up on one elbow, staring at him, absorbing what he was saying, free hand touching his face, memorizing him. "I will always be there for you, okay?" I nodded, suddenly choked up, unable to speak despite my determination to let him go. "Call me, text me. Use a fucking messenger pigeon." I laughed, grateful for the joke. He must have known, even now, what I needed. "I don't care, I will be there. But I have to go and I don't think it's the right move if you come with me."

I met his last word with my lips, kissing him deeply, wanting to remember his taste, his scent, all of it, storing him away for later. When I was satisfied, I looked into those beautiful green eyes.

"I'm going to be fine." And I actually

believed it.

I wanted to stay, but the urge to return home, to write, surprised me. Elliot let me go with a faintly regretful smile and a long, deep kiss. As I walked the block to my place I realized I forgot to tell him about the break in, though fairly certain at this point he knew about my lack ofa job situation. Likely he'd been asked to step back, too, knowing Judy.

None of it seemed important right now.

Weird, that truth. Even more so how calm and still I felt in my thoughts. Was this what Zen felt like? If so, I was all in.

I sat down at my computer, apartment cleaned and orderly around me, and thought about Elliot, the inspiration of our lovemaking. There was no reason to hold back any longer. Inhibitions seemed wasted, tired. There was only my keyboard, and Gabby. Michael. I inhaled, smiled.

And started to write.

CHAPTER THIRTY TWO

I sat at my desk, absorbed in Gabby's world. What was this satisfied feeling that was now my normal? The late Sunday afternoon sun washed out a patch of carpet at my feet, my cup of coffee sitting cold and forgotten in my frenzy of storytelling.

It had been a hell of a week, throwing myself into Gabby's story, her love affair with Michael, and adoring every moment of it. I finished the first draft yesterday afternoon, my frenzy of writing creating that book in a short five days that left me breathless and wanting more. My inner critic's need to judge what I'd created, because surely I couldn't write something of any value in such a short timeframe, died as I delighted in what I'd made. My cheeks tingled while I smiled, pride's gift of excitement filling me with hope. I'd already sent it to Jones, knowing I could trust her to give me what I needed. My bestie was still "dealing with something" as she put it, details not forthcoming. I think maybe I needed to reach out and see if I could help her for once. But I knew without a doubt if Jones needed me she would ask.

She did have time to read my book though, and got back to me this morning.

It's fucking AWESOME! I love it! Her enthusiasm confirmed in me what I already knew. Not that I held back from excited jumping up and down when I got the news.

The surprising delight that came from diving deep? The second day of nonstop writing left me feeling just as satisfied as my time with Elliot, but in a different way. Judy had relented and agreed to call our parting letting me go, assuring I had a severance package and enough security and time to figure out what I wanted to do next. I'd have to get a job eventually, but I owed it to myself to find out what being a writer meant, didn't I?

I knew writers who made extra money selling advertising on their blogs, but they had tons of followers. On impulse, I'd opened my own and, still following instinct, changed the title. *Divorced Life* became *To Mickey, With*

Love. My first post tackled what Elliot and I talked about. Being free and focusing on myself, loving myself. I used E instead of his full name as his identifier, out of a need to protect him, but everything else I let out.

One post led to a daily outpouring, about my life and all the unhappy people in it. How I always thought they were unhappy because of me, taking full responsibility for everything except for myself and my own joy. About Mom, my sister, Richard and the messed up relationships we all chose to continue. About staying in a job I actually hated and about accepting any kind of attention even from sleaze bags because I was starving for love.

Writing it all down felt like saying goodbye and getting the best kind of closure. Talking about my hopes, the spark my writing gave me, was its own post. I owned it, shared my goal to become an author, before posting all of them.

The result? With only a few keywords, my darling little blog now had over a hundred followers already and I was even getting women writing to me about their own journeys. It filled my heart to the brim. This was what I'd always wanted. To make a difference.

I hugged myself, knowing if I could help someone else find freedom, that would be the icing on the cake. I thought of Elliot and my smile grew even bigger. Yes, I missed him already, but I totally understood his decision and thanked him daily for what he'd given me.

As for my old job... I was pretty sure it had been Paul who set me up to be fired. No proof, not anything I could take to someone who might be able to do something about it. But hadn't there been tons of signs along the way?

And the next time I saw him? I was going to thank him for it. I grinned at myself, thinking about the look that would cross his face when instead of telling him off I expressed my gratitude for my freedom.

Mom's text reminded me I was going to be late. Heaven forbid. This was, after all, my final bow in her arena, too. I couldn't miss it and wouldn't for anything.

It was so easy now to reflect, to look around at the people I knew most in my life, to see for the first time how unhappy everyone was. I didn't have to listen to their words. I could recall every word by memory because the conversation never changed. No, I watched intently their interactions, how they were with each other. Richard had found his tablet, though he hadn't forgiven me, that angry moment just a small blip at the beginning of dinner Mom made him discard before sitting down.

Tara had, I noticed then, a similar permanent frown like our mother. I naturally touched my face to make sure I wasn't wearing the same look. Nope, I was good, even forming a grin at the contact. Mom scowled at my expression and I forced my face smooth, though a bubbling giggle threatened to escape. I shouldn't have been enjoying this last supper. But I was.

Oh, I was.

As they talked to each other it was like they chewed their words as much as the tough roast Mom served us. Harsh and cold, judging and weighted by resentment, bitterness, the need to show one another just how much better they were than each other. Sad in so many ways. Their attempted show of perfection stood in such contrast with their demeanor. When I turned my attention back to Richard and Chere I could feel their tension, paid close mind to how they picked at each other. And sadness rose this time.

They wouldn't last, baby or not. How had I ever wanted to be with him? I could smell their unhappiness and knew that had been me, not so long ago, lost in the cloud of hurt and sorrow but unable and unwilling to see the truth. I used to judge myself unworthy because of these people. My awareness hit me deep. I thought there was something wrong with me because they didn't accept me, treated me with disdain.

I actually laughed out loud and pushed away from the table. My mother immediately glared, Tara's lips turning down at the corners.

"What's so funny?" She leveled her index finger at me as I rose and tossed my napkin to the surface of the table. Done, now and forever. "Sit down, young lady. Dinner isn't over."

"Sorry, Mom." I smiled, though without humor, filled with the need to finally be free of who I used to be and using this as my exit to the new me. "It is for me." I walked out of the room, grabbed my coat on the way out the door. I could hear my mother yelling.

"Michaela! Get back here right now!" She hadn't done so the night Richard's reveal drove me out of her apartment. But that had been in my mother's plan, hadn't it? This departure, this was all me and she hated it.

I shut the door, breathing easily where once I'd struggled for air in this place, in my life. As I left the building, I built up steam, joy bubbling, rising, taking me over. Fed by the need to find someone to share these new sensations with.

Freedom was intoxicating. Damn, I wanted a drink.

ABOUT THE AUTHORS

Caron Prins loves the idea of expanding the world's joy through passion and bliss. Co-creating the With Love series was one of those inspirations, her goal to inspire women and men through the written word.

She has worked in the sex toy industry, loves vacationing on nudist resorts and exploring all the titillating deliciousness this beautiful world has to offer. Exotic foods in foreign lands to raves on secluded beaches enjoying new adventures. Life is about exploration, our reason for being. Life is Delicious!

As for Tish Ings, this is a pen name for a prolific, award-winning author who always says yes to her amazing, brave and incredible sister even when it means writing about S-E-X.

Find them and more info on Facebook at www.facebook.com/withloveseries.

www.ingramcontent.com/pod-product-compliance
Lightning Source LLC
Chambersburg PA
CBHW060546180626
46817CB00002B/746